The Home Stand Series
- Book 2 -

By Lacy Hart

Published by Scarlet Lantern Publishing

Copyright © 2019 by
Lacy Hart & Scarlet Lantern Publishing

All rights reserved.

This is a work of fiction. Names, characters, businesses, places, events and incidents are either the products of the author's imagination or used in a fictitious manner. Any resemblance to actual persons, living or dead, or actual events is purely coincidental.

This book contains sexually explicit scenes and adult language.

All characters in this work are 18 years of age or older.

1

The buzz of the alarm cut through the air of the bedroom like a razor and Wes shot up in bed, panting. By the time he calmed down and glanced at the clock, he realized that Kristin must have gotten up early and forgot to turn off the clock on her side of the bed before she left for work. Wes stretched his arm across the bed, still warm from where Kristin slept just a short time ago and slammed the top of the clock to stop the alarm. He saw it was only after seven, and the room was still dark. Sunrise in February in Pennsylvania hadn't happened yet, and it just made Wes feel more like rolling back over to get more sleep. What did he have to get up for anyway, he rationalized. He laid back on his pillow for a moment, staring up into the dark at the ceiling. He could make out the shadow of the ceiling fan in the room, and his eyes adjusted to the dark faster now that he saw a slit of light from the kitchen creeping under the bedroom door.

"Kris?" he yelled, wondering if she was still in the kitchen.

When there was no answer, Wes knew she must have gone out to the library early again. It would take some time for her car to warm up in the cold, but the ride into Chandler to the library was less than five minutes. Why leave so early? *Because she's Kristin,* Wes thought. A smile crept over his lips in the dark. Wes turned to his side, considered going back to sleep, and then sat up in bed. He had been doing too much sleeping in for his liking lately and decided now was as good a time as any to start his day.

The chill of the tiled bathroom floor shot up Wes Martin's spine the moment he placed his foot down on the floor. Moving from the comfort of the shag carpeting of the bedroom to the tile was more than enough to make Wes open his eyes wider. He caught a glimpse of himself in the mirror and saw he was still shaking out the shivers that ran through his body. Wes wasted no time in turning the shower on and getting it as hot as he knew he could stand before stripping off his flannel bottoms and climbing into the stall. The hot water pelted his muscles and worked through the cold his body tried to hold onto.

Wes sighed deeply and rested both palms flat on the shower wall in front of him so the hot water could continue to work its magic. The water dripped from his brown hair, letting Wes know that his hair was much longer than it would have been back in his baseball playing days when it was short and neat. He hadn't seen much of the need to keep up with things like that, and a quick rub of his chin made him realize he had more than just a day or two of stubble on his face. It was far from the norm for him, but Wes hadn't been inclined to worry about things like this much for the last six months or so.

When he finished showering, Wes climbed out and heard the familiar pop that his left knee often made in the mornings. Stiffness in the knee he had surgery on more than a year ago was something he dealt with more now as well, especially since working out was no longer a daily obligation. Wes flexed the knee back and forth a few times to work the kinks out, hoping the tightness would go away quickly, but Wes knew that from the way his knee had been for the last few weeks that wasn't likely to happen. Ever since he had slipped and fallen in the driveway when he chased his daughter Isabelle playfully as they tossed snowballs at each other, his knee hadn't felt right. The idea of trudging to Pittsburgh to see his orthopedist made Wes shake his head to erase the thought. The ride took too long, and he never knew who he might run into while he was there. The Pirates still used the orthopedist as one of their primary doctors and having to see ex-teammates who would inevitably ask him what retirement was like, how he was doing, and if he missed the game was not something he looked forward to.

Wrapped only in his towel, Wes sat on the edge of the bed. He glanced to his right and caught a glimpse of himself in the full-length mirror in the corner of the room. He stood up from the bed, his knee groaning again, and walked until he was in front of the mirror. The flecks of gray that dotted his brown hair were becoming more visible. His gaze worked its way down, and he saw that he was still fit, thanks mainly to all the chores done around the horse farm, but it wasn't like it was when he was playing, and he was proudest of his physique.

Wes went to his dresser and mindlessly pulled out clothes for the day. Before he pulled his jeans on, he moved back to his dresser and grabbed the sleeve that slid over his knee that helped give it extra support. He had been wearing it frequently lately, trying to hide it from Kristin when he could so she wouldn't worry about him and coerce him into seeing the doctor. Trying to convince Kristin that it was nothing to be concerned about might be a battle he didn't want to fight just yet. Wes held out hope the knee would start to feel better with some stretching, and when the warmer weather of the spring might finally get here in a month or so.

Wes paced out of the bedroom to the kitchen and saw the stainless-steel coffee carafe sitting on the counter with a pink sticky note attached to it. Wes pulled the letter off to read it.

Got up early to drive Izzy to school. Auditions for the spring musical were this morning, and she was keyed up. I left you some coffee. How about lunch today? Let me know.

Love you,

Kris

Wes had forgotten about the spring musical auditions, even though he shouldn't have since it was all Izzy had been talking about for the last week or so. She had been up in her room practicing with every free moment, listening to the soundtrack from "The Little Mermaid." It had gotten to the point where Wes and Kristin now knew all the words to the songs as well, and more than once Wes received weird looks from his Dad when they worked on the farm and Wes would find himself singing "Kiss the Girl" in a deep, calypso style voice.

The fresh aroma of the coffee emanated from the carafe the moment Wes started pouring, and the smell alone was enough for Wes to perk up. He took a few quick sips as he strode towards the back doors and opened the blinds. The sun was just starting to peek up now, and it could be seen just beyond the rise in the hill at the rear of the house out towards the back building.

Wes stared out not so much at the sunrise, but at that building. He hadn't been up there since the month after he retired. The building held the indoor batting cage he had constructed years ago so that he could train during the off-season. Wes spent hours up there on many occasions. He hit ball after ball until there were blisters underneath his batting gloves, as he looked to perfect his swing against curveballs with wicked breaks or fastballs that moved at ninety-five miles per hour or more. All that extra training had paid off for him over the years, but now the building served only as a memory of what was. More than once, Wes thought about finding another use for the space, but he never had the heart to go beyond those initial feelings.

It took just a few more sips of his coffee before Wes knew his plan for this morning. He didn't have any chores he had to get to right away on the farm, and since he got up and about earlier than usual, why not go up there? He walked back into the bedroom and took off his jeans, replacing them with a pair of black sweatpants. He put his boots on and grabbed a pair of sneakers from the closet while he pulled out his red flannel jacket. The building was only in the backyard, but a good four inches of snow covered the ground, with ice likely underneath that, and the temperature had barely been above twenty degrees lately.

That first step out onto the back porch gave the familiar crunch Wes always loved as a kid. He constantly wanted to be the first one to step into the snow outside, even if it meant he had to shovel off the front porch and sidewalk for his parents. Wes made sure to move gingerly as he went across the yard and scaled the incline to the building. The last thing he wanted to do was fall, wrench his knee, and have to explain to Kristin, Izzy, his parents, the paramedics, or anyone else just what he was trying to do.

The incline seemed steeper than he remembered, and Wes saw his labored breath hang in the cold air with each step before he reached the door of the batting cage. Before he went inside, he made sure to go over to the switch box outside and turn the power back on. He had shut the electricity off months ago since it wasn't getting any use. Wes turned the key in the lock and kicked away some of the snow that had built up outside the door so he could pull it open enough to step inside.

The inside of the building contained the same frosty chill as the outside. Wes flipped the light switch, and the lights flickered on. He noticed a few of the fluorescents high up on the ceiling were out, but there was no way he was getting the equipment up here from the farm to change the lights until a good spring thaw. Besides, he figured on just taking a few swings to get it out of his system, and then he would not be back up here again for months, if ever.

Wes unzipped his jacket and hung it on one of the hooks just inside the door in an old baseball locker he purchased from a collector years ago. It was an old locker from Forbes Field, and Wes imagined all the greats like Clemente and Mazeroski used the locker at some point. With his jacket off and just a t-shirt on, Wes could see the hair on his arm, along with the accompanying goosebumps, as they came to life from the cold. He went over to the thermostat on the far wall and turned the temperature up to 72, but he knew he might complete the workout before the heat came up to anywhere near being warm.

Wes had spared no expense in keeping the batting cage up to state-of-the-art, and a remote and a computer controlled everything. He turned on the computer and picked up the remote for the pitching machine, pressing the button and aiming to turn the device on. The machine whirred and hummed as it came to life, and Wes saw the lights of the machine flicker on from sixty feet, six inches away. Excitement coursed through his veins, and he waited with anticipation for the computer to finish booting so he could start.

A few strides away was the bat rack, covered with a gray tarp. Wes peeled back the cover and picked up the first bat on the rack. It had always been one of his favorites, and he slowly ran his hand over the wood. All his bats were always made of maple, and he long had a deal with Louisville Slugger to supply his bats. They had been his favorites since he was in high school and he never wavered over the years even as younger players came along and went with ash or other types of woods and other companies. Wes' thumb grazed over the imprint of his name on the bat, and he got that familiar rush.

The beep of the pitching machine pushed Wes out of his haze, and he glanced up to see that the green light on the device glowed, indicating its readiness for use. Wes returned to the locker and pulled on a pair of batting gloves, adjusting the Velcro several times to get the fit just right. He considered going into the cage without a helmet but thought better of it. It had been too long, and one mishit could leave him lying unconscious on the floor where no one would find him for days. He still had one of his old Pirates' helmets and chose that one to wear. The helmet fit tighter than expected, mainly because of the extra hair on Wes' head instead of the buzz cut he regularly wore during the playing season.

A stop at the computer before he entered the cage so it could track results happened first, and then Wes revisited familiar territory. He stood in the batter's box next to the faux home plate and tapped it lightly three times with the top of the bat. The computer called balls and strikes for him as they hit the net behind him since the machine was set up to replicate real-life pitching, and Wes looked back at the netting and gave a nod, just as he would when he stepped in, and a real umpire occupied that spot. He grabbed the remote and pointed it at the pitcher, pressing the start button.

Wes dug in with his right foot, shuffling into the imaginary dirt beneath him. He took a few brief practice swings before the first pitch began its way towards him. He found himself flailing at a curveball that he didn't expect, nearly falling across the batter's box as the ball hit the net. The next pitch came in as a rising fastball, and he fared no better with that one. In fact, the first ten pitches he saw he either swung and missed or let go, only to see them rung up as strikes. The eleventh pitch moved quickly, an inside fastball that he barely tipped, just enough to have it ricochet off his right ankle.

"Fuck!" Wes yelled in anger, and he slammed the bat down. He angrily pressed the pause button on the pitching machine and hobbled out of the cage over to the locker where he had a chair to sit on. He rolled up the pant leg of his sweats and gently tugged down his sock to a bruise darkening just above his ankle. Wes reached over to a shelf in the locker where he kept some supplies and grabbed a spray bottle of ethyl chloride. He shot a few cold sprays onto his leg, shivered, and pulled his sock back up.

The rational part of his brain told Wes to put the bat back, turn the machine off and go back to the nice, warm house, and have another cup of coffee. The baseball player in him, however, said *to hell with that,* picked up the bat, and got back in the cage. Wes breathed deeply, pressed the pause button again, and the device lit up as it readied another pitch. He squinted out towards the pitcher as his hands gripped tightly around the bat handle. In an instant, the next pitch was upon him, and Wes let loose with a hellacious swing. He felt the reverberation of the bat on ball as his eyes followed the swing all the way through and the ball took off high into the net well at the other end of the cage.

A tremendous feeling of satisfaction surged through him, and pitch after pitch from there on got sent back in the form of line drives or high flies that might go out of most stadiums. Wes kept it up, hitting everything served up at him until he was bathed in sweat from head to toe. After Wes sent one curveball that screamed back on a line ten feet over the pitching device, he turned the machine off, satisfied with his efforts. He exited the cage and went back over to sit down at the locker. Wes peeled off the batting gloves and picked up his bat. He could feel the warm spots where his hands gripped the handle and the marks on the wood from all the balls he had hit. He held the bat under his nose and inhaled, taking in the sweet odor of the warm maple.

"God, I miss this," Wes whispered, almost afraid that someone would hear him say it out loud.

2

The ice that built upon the windows of the Jeep was much more than Kristin and Izzy expected that morning. Both worked furiously on the front window, chiseling through that glacier-like layer as if they were furious sculptors looking to get through marble. Both were red-faced when they hopped into the front seats of the car, waiting for the defroster to work its magic on what was left on the windshield. Kristin flicked on the headlights to cut through the dark morning before the sun had come up.

"Boy, I really hope you get this part, Izzy," Kristin said, as her gloves gripped the steering wheel and her boots danced furiously on the floor mats as she anxiously awaited the defroster to complete its mission so she could switch the heat on. Kristin was grateful that Wes insisted she dispose of her old car last year, the one that she treasured for years through college and beyond. She knew it was on its last legs with each repair done, and after six months of being with Wes, he went out and bought her a new Jeep Cherokee as a sort of anniversary present. Kristin insisted it was too much, but Wes made the argument that she needed to be safe driving around Chandler, whether it was just her, Izzy, or anyone else.

"I think I have the best shot, thanks to you," Izzy replied, taking off her plaid ski cap and shaking out her long hair that Kristin dyed red for her last night after Wes went to bed.

"You better, or your father is going to kill both of us for that hair dye in the bathroom."

"The only other girl who has a shot is Allison Marx, and she has black hair. I think the red hair will put me over the top." Izzy pulled down the passenger-side visor and glanced in the small mirror, smiling as she gazed at her red locks.

Once the rear window was clear, Kristin started the trek down the winding driveway, making sure to carefully go over the snow-ice combination that resided. She glided past Wes' parents' house, seeing the living room light on since Wyatt was likely up having his coffee and getting ready to head down to the stables.

Kristin eased out onto Route 5 and made her way towards Chandler High School, which was just a few minutes away. Izzy already plugged her iPod in and sang along with "Part of Your World," emoting as best she could with each line. Kristin had been impressed the first time she heard Izzy start to sing around the house, but Izzy had clearly gotten even better over the weeks as she prepared for auditions. Kristin found herself joining in, singing with Izzy as loud as she could, even though she knew she was a bit off-key. When the song ended, the two looked at each other and laughed.

When they reached the school, Izzy practically had the car door opened before the Jeep even came to a full stop. Other cars dropped off students for auditions or early classes, and students hustled into the school to avoid the early morning biting wind that kicked up.

"Hey!" Kristin yelled to Izzy as the teenager stepped out of the car, grabbing her backpack off the floor. Izzy looked up abruptly to see what was wrong.

"Good luck in there," Kristin said with a smile. "I know you can do it."

Izzy leaned back in the car and gave Kristin a big hug.

"Thanks, Kris… for everything." Izzy gave Kristin a quick peck on the cheek and dashed out of the car towards the front doors of the school. Kristin watched as Izzy entered before she pulled away and headed back towards the center of Chandler so she could get to the library.

The entire ride in (all five minutes of it), Kristin thought about how far her relationship with Izzy came in just a year. When she first met Izzy at Izzy's grandparents' house when she delivered a book for Izzy to read to her grandmother, Kristin was simply Ms. Arthur, the town librarian. Over a short time, when her relationship with Wes Martin began, Izzy turned initially resentful. The two became much closer over the year, and now Kristin felt that they were not only close friends but more like sisters. Kristin turned out to be the female presence in Izzy's life that Izzy missed, and the two bonded over everything, sometimes to the dismay of Wes as he navigated the world of a teenage girl.

Kristin pulled into her usual parking spot at the library and moved to the front doors as fast as she could to unlock them. It was much earlier than when the library opened to the public, but the early morning quiet never became lost on her. She loved to enter the library, settle down, organize, and plan out the day without any interruptions on the phone or by visitors to the library. Mornings like this gave her a chance to gather her thoughts, and Kristin often got her best ideas on days like this.

She made a lot of progress in the year or so as the head librarian, introducing new community programs, getting guest speakers, updating the computers and lending system, and even getting the library board to agree to some expansion to help the facility grow. It meant a lot of time and effort, some begging and pleading for donors, and hours doing book sales, tricky trays, raffles, and all kinds of other fundraisers, but Kristin made it happen and never felt prouder of herself.

The lights in the library came to a glow when Kristin flipped the switch, and she moved right to the thermostat to turn the heat up slightly to take the chill out of the room before people arrived in a few hours. Kristin then walked to her office, dropped her leather bag next to her desk, and turned her computer on. She sat back and watched as it came to life, signed in and then spied the wallpaper of the picture of Wes and herself seated at the picnic table down by the pond on the farm, the site of one of their first dates.

Kristin switched out of her winter boots and into her low heels and then hung up her coat on the coat rack in the corner. The weather proved to be far too cold lately for skirts and dresses, so she opted for a sensible black pair of slacks today and one of her favorite sweaters, light green with a V-neck that complemented both her eyes and her figure. Kristin sat at her desk and clicked open her email, just browsing through to see if anything required an immediate answer. A few speaker confirmations and book requests and questions appeared, but beyond that, nothing that couldn't wait or be deleted.

Kristin scanned the latest local and national news as she took time for herself. She noticed a small blurb in the news section about today being the first day of spring training for the Pirates. Kristin had become a baseball fan, by association at first since it was Wes' livelihood and passion, but now she found herself with an avid interest in the game. However, she forgot about spring training starting already. Worry crossed her mind as she thought about how Wes might handle it.

Kristin always felt that part of Wes sorely missed playing baseball. It clearly fulfilled his life, and even though Wes insisted that he gave it up because he was ready to get on with the next portion of his life, Kristin harbored a bit of a guilty feeling that he walked away after an explosive few games with a new team just to come back and be with her. Kristin loved Wes with all her heart and was ecstatic that he was there for her, but she also didn't want him to live with any regrets. She mentioned that to Wes a few times throughout last season, especially when a few teams came calling with hopes to coax Wes out of retirement for the stretch run towards the playoffs. She was shocked when he turned down a lucrative offer from the Red Sox, who hunted for a DH, but Wes said no right away. They watched the Red Sox together as Boston team won the World Series again, and Kristin asked Wes regarding any second thoughts about turning the team down when he could have won a World Series ring.

"Not even for a minute," he told her with a big smile as he took her in his arms and kissed her passionately.

Kristin occupied herself with chores around the library for the two hours before her associate and closest friend, Karen Manning, would come in for work. Kristin made a pot of coffee, checked in the books that dropped in the depository overnight, organized items on the shelf, and even cleaned up the kids' play area, cleaning the tables and vacuuming the rug there. By the time Karen walked through the door at 8:30, the place sparkled, and the aroma of coffee permeated the entire library.

"Someone had too much time this morning," Karen said as she took off her coat and hung it on the coat rack.

"Good morning to you, too," Kristin said with a smile, handing Karen a cup filled with the Costa Rican blend Kristin brewed this morning. Karen inhaled the scent hovering over the mug and smiled.

"Hmmm, come to Mama," she quipped as she sipped. "What got into you this morning?" Karen asked.

"Izzy had to be at school early for auditions, so I took her in and came right here. I hope everything went well for her. I thought she would have texted me right away about it."

"I'm sure she'll let you know," Karen reassured her. "You are such a worrying mother now."

"I am not," Kristin said defensively. "I'm not her mother, Karen, and I try not to pretend to be or think of myself that way. I think we're more like good friends."

"Be honest, Kris," Karen sat on her stool at the main desk. "You have never thought about what it would be like if you and Wes got married and you become her stepmom? Marriage has never crossed your mind?"

Kristin stared back at Karen, frozen. Marrying Wes crossed her mind, but it was not something she and Wes even discussed at this point. It had been almost a year since they were together, and as close as they were, Kristin did not want to feel like she pressured Wes into anything. She was still young, only twenty-three now, but she didn't imagine a future where Wes and Izzy weren't a part of it.

"Of course it's crossed my mind," Kristin told Karen as Kristin paced the floor a bit and looked for the right words to say. "Everybody thinks about marriage when they are in a long-term relationship, but it isn't something we talked about at all."

"You gave up your apartment to live with him, Kris. You do everything together; you love and help take care of his daughter and family; it's almost like you are married already. I'm just surprised you haven't talked about it is all."

"Well, what about you and Brian?" Kristin said to her, hoping to divert some of the pressure and focus. "Have you two talked about marriage? You've dated just as long as Wes and me."

"As a matter of fact, we have," Karen said with a big grin, as she held out her left hand and wiggled her fingers so that the engagement ring on her hand sparkled in the light.

Kristin gasped as she moved towards Karen, who had jumped out of her chair to meet Kristin.

"Karen, that's unbelievable!" Kristin shouted. Kristin took Karen's hand and held it up so she could get a closer look at the princess cut diamond she sported on her ring finger. "When did he ask you? And why didn't you call me right after?"

"It happened last night," Karen proudly stated. "We sat in his apartment watching a movie, and he called his dog Rascal over to come to sit with us. Rascal sat next to me and had this little box tied in a ribbon around his collar, and the ring was in there. It was adorable. Then Brian got down on one knee and proposed. I would have called you right after but… we… we were a little busy," Karen added with a salacious grin.

"Okay, I forgive you for not calling," Kristin said as she embraced Karen. "Congratulations. I'm so happy for you. Have you thought about when the wedding will be?"

"Brian wants to get married sooner rather than later," Karen added excitedly. "I think he's worried I'll change my mind," she laughed. "We were talking about some time in the spring if we can pull it together."

"The spring?" Kristin said, shocked. "That only gives you a couple of months to plan everything."

"I know." Karen walked back over to her stool, sat down, and picked up her coffee mug. "I guess I can start right now by asking you to be my maid of honor."

Karen beamed over her coffee mug and watched as Kristin broke out in a smile.

"Of course, I will," Kristin told her.

"Thank God, because I don't know anyone who is as organized as you and can help me get all this arranged."

A hard rap on the front door caught their attention, and Kristin glanced down at her watch and saw it was a bit after nine, past opening time. She hustled over to the front door to unlock it and let in Mrs. Pauling, an older woman who frequented the library. Mrs. Pauling huffed a bit as she entered.

"It's ten past, you know," she said to Kristin. "I practically froze to death out there waiting for you to open the door."

"I'm sorry, Mrs. Pauling," Kristin offered. "We just got caught up. Karen just told me she got engaged last night." Kristin followed Mrs. Pauling into the main library, and they both looked at a smiling Karen.

"Hmmph," Mrs. Pauling grumbled. "People get engaged all the time. It doesn't mean you open the doors late." Mrs. Pauling worked her way over to the new release section opposite the front desk and started browsing. As soon she turned her back, Karen stuck her tongue out at her. Kristin did all she could to stifle a laugh.

"Something funny?" Mrs. Pauling said as she shot Kristin a look.

"No ma'am," Kristin replied, scurrying behind the front desk towards her office. "Good luck with her today," she whispered to Karen, rolling her eyes.

"Even that old grouch can't bring me down today," Karen answered.

Kristin walked back into her office and sat at her desk. She smiled and felt happy for Karen, but part of her panged with more than a little jealousy, even though she wouldn't admit it. Just then, her phone buzzed with a text from Izzy.

Nailed it!! TTYL

A picture of Izzy, smiling into the camera, her red hair flowing and her blue eyes shimmering, filled her phone screen. The audition obviously went well.

The day seemed to have gotten off to a nice start for a lot of people, and Kristin hoped in her heart that she would be a part of that good fortune as well. She sighed and looked back at the wallpaper on her computer, staring at the image of her and Wes.

3

After spending the better part of an hour swinging at pitches in the batting cage, Wes exhausted himself. He achieved such a good rhythm after struggling from the start that he feared to stop, worried the good swings would somehow vanish into thin air. He shut the pitching machine down, toweled off and sat for a while, and then looked at the computer screen that charted his swing statistics for him. He saw that his contact steadily improved, launch angle rose, and exit velocity was better than he thought it would be. Wes laughed and shook his head, knowing that when the company that installed the system explained how it could chart all these things for him, he scoffed about how unimportant they were. Now, in the state of baseball, these analytics were what GMs and front offices looked at the most. Even if he was considered a "dinosaur" or "old man" at thirty-seven, Wes knew his stats needed to compete with kids who weren't much older than his daughter.

Wes spent some time cleaning up the area, putting baseballs away, checking machinery, and doing chores he hadn't done up there in many months to keep the cage ready for the next time he wanted to use it. He already decided there would be more, and he even began to map out a workout schedule that might help him get in better shape and get that muscle memory up where he needed it.

When he stepped outside and locked up, Wes quickly remembered that it was February in Pennsylvania and not Bradenton, Florida. The sweat that formed on him quickly chilled and froze over, clinging to his hair and making it stiff. He worked his way down the hill back towards the house gingerly, realizing that getting up the hill with the snow and ice on the ground proved easier than trying to work his way down. The small slip he took as he neared the bottom caused his right leg to slide out in front of him and turn, and his brain swiftly recalled the blow his ankle had taken from a ball a bit ago. Wes fell and slid down the rest of the way towards the house. As much as he tried to stop the skid, his hands could do little in the snow and ice until his body reached the level surface just beyond the back patio.

  Wes lay back on the ground for a few moments. His head rested in the skid mark it had made in the snow while his right leg was up on a small mound it created as his body worked its way down the hill. His first thoughts were about potential injury to his surgically repaired knee, and then to his back, before the dull ache in his ankle returned with a flourish. Wes sat up, still feeling the pain, and scooted himself through the snow onto the patio where he could grasp the edge of one of the tables that were covered up for the winter. He hoisted himself up and braced against the table for a moment before he put his right leg down to make sure it could support his weight. Pain shot up his leg and caused a grimace.

  The back door lurked like a life preserver in the water for Wes, and thankfully Wes had the forethought to shovel off the back patio a few days ago, so there was a clear path to get there. The tricky part came when he found he needed to hop to the door, to keep his ankle off the ground as he tried not to fall again. He lunged the last foot or two and grabbed the door handle, turning it so he could get into the kitchen. Wes used every piece of furniture within his reach to traverse through the room and then took a few big hops into the bedroom before he leaped for the bed. Once on the bed, Wes huffed as sweat poured from him, almost as much as right after his workout in the batting cages. He pushed further up the mattress so he could reach his nightstand and then grabbed his cell phone. His first instinct was to call Kristin, but he changed his mind before he could press the button to dial her. Instead, he called down to his parents' house, dialing his father's phone. After a few rings, Wyatt answered.

"Hey there," his father replied. "You didn't come down for breakfast this morning. Sleeping in again? There's plenty of work to do in the stables if you need something to occupy your time."

"Funny, Dad," Wes said. "Look, I need your help. I took a little fall, and I think I hurt myself."

"Are you alright?"

"Dad, if I were alright, I wouldn't be calling you for help," Wes said with exasperation. "It feels like my ankle."

"Well, Dr. Emerson is here checking up on your Mom. I can run up with him if you want."

Wes didn't want this to be more of a big deal than he thought it was but having the doctor check it out seemed like a good idea.

"That would be perfect," Wes said. "Could you please not mention anything to Mom? I… I don't want her to worry about me."

When he said this, Wes knew it wasn't entirely right. Sure, he didn't want his mother to worry. She had her own illness and battles to fight. Wes' more significant concern lay with his Mom saying something in front of Kristin, who would then wonder what happened.

"Sure, no problem. We'll be up in a minute."

"Thanks, Dad."

Wes hung up and tossed the phone back on the bed next to him. He glanced at the clock on his nightstand and saw it was nearly ten, and then remembered Kristin's note this morning about meeting her for lunch. Kristin usually went to lunch around noon and meeting her in town today seemed less and less like a reality.

A moment later, Wes heard the front door open and close.

"Wes?" his father's voice yelled.

"In my bedroom Dad," Wes shouted.

Wyatt Martin entered his son's bedroom, sauntering in just like a cowboy swinging through saloon doors. His wiry frame deceived many, as he remained stronger and quicker than most men half his age. His thick, gray mustache lent even more to his cowboy look, and he smiled as he came into the room.

"What did you do now?" Wyatt spoke, sounding to Wes just like he had when Wes got injured often as a teenager.

Dr. Emerson followed close behind Wyatt. A man also in his sixties much like Wyatt, Dr. Emerson didn't carry nearly the same fitness level of his cowboy counterpart. Phil Emerson carried a slight paunch, a lot less hair, and rolled into the room more than strode.

"I slipped and fell, Dad. Hi Dr. Emerson," Wes noted, nodding to the doctor as he sat on the edge of the bed. "I think I hurt my right ankle."

"Let's take a look," Dr. Emerson said as he gently removed Wes' sock and rolled up Wes' pant leg to his knee. One glance down at the ankle and the sight of the large black and blue egg there from the baseball strike gave Dr. Emerson and Wyatt pause.

"You got that from a fall?" Wyatt said. "Did you fall off the roof?"

Wes' face flushed as he thought of a way to explain things to his father.

"No, the bruise came from… well, I had gone up to the batting cage and took some swings. I fouled one off my ankle, and it got me good. But then I fell coming down the hill on my way back, and I think I made it worse."

Wyatt nodded at his son as Dr. Emerson examined Wes' ankle, feeling around it and his foot, before working his way up his leg to his knee.

"Anything else hurt, Wes?" the doctor inquired.

"Just his pride, I'm guessing," Wyatt answered, arching his eyebrow at Wes.

Wes shot a look towards his father before he turned his attention back to Dr. Emerson. "No, everything else feels okay."

"I think it's just a pretty nasty bruise, Wes, and you may have turned your ankle a bit when you slid. If you want, you can come down to the office, and we can check it out further – x-rays, and such – but I don't think we'll find anything else."

"No, that's not necessary," Wes answered immediately.

"For now, just put some ice on it, take some pain reliever, and keep it elevated. If it doesn't feel any better, call my office and let me know. We'll have you come down to look at it again."

"Thanks, Doc," Wes said, smiling as he tried to sit up some more.

"I'll see him out and get you an ice pack," Wyatt told Wes as Wyatt motioned Wes to stay on the bed.

Wes propped up a few pillows behind him and then slid one underneath his right foot. Even just grazing his ankle with the soft down made him wince.

Wyatt reentered the room, holding one of the ice wraps that Wes always kept in the freezer for when he needed one for the various bumps and bruises he always seemed to have. Wyatt wrapped the pack around the ankle, using the Velcro straps on it to close it. Chills went up Wes' spine as the cold rested against the bruise.

Wes felt the look his father gave him and tried to divert Wyatt's attention.

"How's Mom?" Wes asked.

"Phil says she's doing okay. You know how it is. She's supposed to be careful about what she does and where she goes, and she never pays much mind to that, so she wears herself out, gets sick, and we start worrying all over again. She just needs to relax and use her oxygen concentrator more. Now, how about you? Why did you go up to the batting cage knowing there was nothing but snow and ice out there?"

"I don't know, Dad. I looked out the back doors at the building, and thought I hadn't been up there in a while, and…" Wes' voice trailed off.

"And you realized this was the week spring training starts in Florida," Wyatt told him decisively.

"Yeah," Wes answered sheepishly. "I just wanted to see what it would feel like. It's been months since I even picked up a bat."

"What did you prove to yourself?" Wyatt sat down next to him on the bed.

"It took me a little bit, but my swings were good, maybe even better than good," Wes told his father. "Consistent contact, my launch angle and exit speed were better than I hoped, and I drove the ball."

"Okay," Wyatt answered as he rubbed his stubbled chin. "What does all that mean to you?"

"It just means I can still hit, and maybe…"

"Where are you going with this Wes? Are you thinking about trying to go back to baseball?"

"I don't know, Dad," Wes told him honestly. "Part of me misses it… misses it a lot. I think if I spent some time getting myself back into better shape and worked at it that maybe Randy could get me an invite to spring training with someone. I don't know if I could make it or not, but I might like to try."

"How long have you been feeling this way?"

"On and off for about a month or so, I guess," Wes replied.

"Does Kristin know about this?" Wyatt had genuine concern in his voice now.

Wes sighed. "No, I haven't mentioned it to her yet, and I don't know if I am going to, so please don't say anything to her, Dad. Maybe this is just a passing thing, pangs because my body is used to going to spring training this time of year every year for the last eighteen years or so. I don't know what it is, and until I do, I don't want to say anything to her or Izzy."

"Wes, you know me. I'll respect your wishes, but I'm not going to lie for you either. If they ask me about it, I'm going to be honest with them. It's up to you to be straight about all this. Kristin loves you. She deserves to know what you're feeling. You're in this together, right?"

"Of course, we are," Wes shot back. "How could you think anything else? I love her with all my heart."

"Then let her know what's going on," Wyatt said as he stood up.

Wes' cell phone rang, startling both men. Wes reached over and picked it up, seeing it was Kristin.

"Hi," Wes said as he switched rapidly to a chipper tone.

"Hey there," Kristin replied. "I hadn't heard from you, so I thought I'd call and see if you were coming down for lunch today. I left so early this morning, I'm already famished, and I'd love to see you."

"I'd love to see you too," Wes answered, as he looked down at his steadily numbing ankle. "But I don't know, I'm pretty tired today. I guess I didn't sleep well or something. Can I take a rain check?"

"Of course, you can," Kristin said. "Go take a nap and relax. I can pick up some Chinese for dinner on my way home if you want so you don't have to worry about a thing. It's probably a good idea to do that anyway. I'm sure Izzy is going to want to tell us all about her audition this morning."

"Great." Wes felt more at ease now that he knew he had a few more hours to recuperate his ankle before anyone got home. "I'll see you later then."

"You bet," Kristin said to him. "I love you."

"Love you too," Wes replied, and hung up, and then looked up at his father, who leered back at him. Wyatt heard the conversation and gave a disapproving look.

"I don't like where this is going," Wyatt said, as he sauntered towards the bedroom door.

4

Wes spent most of the afternoon alternating ice on and off his ankle, to get the swelling down quite a bit, but the purple and black speckled bruise that formed showed no signs of fading at all, and the bruise remained tender to the touch. He hopped off the bed tentatively, just to put the toes on his right foot down at first to see if he experienced any pain. All felt well, and he put full weight down. His heel hit the floor, and a dull ache spread across the top of his foot and up his leg. The pain, while still present, improved to a tolerable level.

All of Wes' years playing baseball helped to toughen him to injuries like bruises, scrapes, strains, and sprains. Wes managed to tolerate them well and learned treatment regimens from trainers over the years that helped ease injuries so he could play through them. The lessons he learned would see him through this one, but having been away from baseball for so long now left him a little concerned about how quickly he could bounce back. More of a concern was what Kristin and Izzy would think about the injury and how he got it.

Wes resolved to walk around as much as he could put up with before the girls got home, and hoped that he would at least have something of a normal gait before they arrived. He did a few laps around the main level of the house, going from the kitchen to the living room and dining room and back again, working his way around furniture and holding onto the backs of the dining chairs for stability when he felt he needed it. When it got close to five, and he knew Kristin and Izzy would be home soon, he went back into the bedroom, put his dirty clothes into the hamper so Kristin wouldn't see the damp pants with the stains on them from when he slid down the hill and went to the kitchen to set the table for the Chinese food they were bringing home.

Wes turned the music speaker on so he could listen while he set out plates and cutlery. He heard the front door open and close, and the familiar voices and giggling from Izzy and Kristin filled the house and brought a smile to his face. He relished the happy sounds that he heard, knowing that the girls became so close over the last year.

Wes turned as Kristin entered the kitchen and held up the brown paper bag that brimmed with food. The smell of the fried wrappers of egg rolls that were clearly on top of the bag overwhelmed the usual aroma of the room. Kristin smiled and walked over to the table. She placed the bag in the center and then stood on her tiptoes to give Wes a gentle kiss on the lips.

"Dinner is served," she laughed.

"Where's Izzy?" Wes asked, looking around for his daughter. "I heard her talking to you when you came in."

"Oh, she ran upstairs to drop off her stuff before coming down to eat. Wes, there's something I need to tell you before Izzy gets down here…"

Kristin hoped to let Wes know that she helped Izzy dye her hair for her auditions, but before she could say anything, Izzy had bounded into the kitchen, her long, now red hair bouncing along with her. Wes' stare followed Izzy from the doorway to the table and never wavered.

"Hi Dad," Izzy said, kissing his cheek. "How was your day?"

Izzy plopped herself down in a chair and dug into the bag of food, pulling out the package of egg rolls to take one and put it on her plate. She took a quick bite and crunched as she proceeded to take the rest of the food out of the bag. She placed the plastic containers around the table in a diamond pattern and smiled at her handiwork.

All the while, Wes stared, and then his view moved over to Kristin, who saw the puzzled look on his face.

"What happened to your hair?" Wes asked.

Izzy looked up and tried to swallow before she spoke.

"It's red for the tryouts. Ariel has red hair, Dad. I wanted to get into character as much as I could to really give myself a shot. Do you like it?" Izzy tossed her hair a bit and laughed. She picked up her egg roll and dipped into the duck sauce she had squirted on her plate, spreading the sauce so that the egg roll dripped of bright orange before she took another bite.

"But what if you don't get the part?" Wes stated. "Then you have bright red hair like this for who knows how long. Do you think that's a good idea?"

Izzy peered over at Kristin, waiting for support to kick in to help her with her father.

"It's fine, Wes, really," Kristin said, as she rested a hand on Wes' shoulder. "I think she looks good with red hair anyway. Izzy, tell your Dad how the auditions went." Kristin sat down and poured some of the won ton soup from the quart container into a bowl in front of her plate. She swirled the spoon around, waiting for Izzy to explain how tryouts played out.

"Fabulous!" Izzy stated. Izzy inadvertently sprayed small bits of cabbage out of her mouth as she spoke. Izzy laughed heartily as some landed squarely on Wes' t-shirt. He glanced down and then back over at Izzy, who picked up a napkin and wiped Wes' shirt before she wiped her own mouth.

"Sorry, Dad." Izzy balled up the napkin and put it next to her plate. "The auditions went great. I nailed my song and Miss Baker, one of the assistants with the show, told me she thought I sang the best of the group. They announce the cast soon, so I have my fingers crossed."

"That's great honey," Wes said, still not fully accepting the flaming red hair sitting across from him. "I'm proud of you. I hope you get it."

The three sat and ate, working their way through General Tso's chicken, fried rice, and chicken and broccoli until only empty containers dotted the table. Kristin and Izzy both told Wes about their days, but Wes hardly acknowledged the details of what they spoke about. His mind constantly shifted back to what he did wrong while batting today and how much better he thought he could be tomorrow with just some minor adjustments to his swing.

"Wes?" Kristin shouted, snapping Wes out of his daze.

"I'm sorry, what?" Wes said, lightly shaking his head.

"I asked if you were done. Are you feeling okay? I know you said you weren't earlier today." Kristin flashed a concerned look on her face.

"I think I'm just tired today," Wes said with a slight smile. He rose from his seat and began to pick up the empty containers.

"I can put this stuff in the dishwasher," Kristin told him. "Why don't you just go lay down for a bit."

"Thanks, I think I will." Wes kissed Kristin on top of her head and then did the same to Izzy, who was still seated at the table as she polished off what was left of the fried rice on her plate.

"Nice job today, kiddo," Wes crowed before he shuffled off to the bedroom.

Izzy looked up at Kristin as she finished her food.

"Is Dad okay?" Izzy asked. Izzy grabbed her plate and cutlery and headed over to the dishwasher. "He seems kind of out of it today. Do you think he was freaked out about my hair?"

"I think he's alright, Izzy," Kristin answered. "I think it's just…" Kristin crept closer to Izzy. "It's just the time of year is all," she whispered. "This was always when spring training started for him, and I think he's a little down about it and missing it."

"Geez, I didn't even remember about it." Izzy glanced at Wes' bedroom door, which was now closed. "And I just went on and on about all I was doing while we ate. Now I feel like a jerk."

"Hey, it's nothing to feel bad about," Kristin reassured. "You should be proud of your achievements and what you are doing, and you should be happy to share them, especially with your father."

"Thanks, Kris," Izzy said. She finished loading the dishwasher and pushed the door shut until it latched. "I'm going up to my room, do some homework, and then talk to Amy about auditions."

Alone in the kitchen, Kristin went to the refrigerator and pulled out the half bottle of Pinot Grigio that was still in there. Reaching two glasses from the overhead rack while she stood on her tiptoes - *I have to remember to ask Wes to move this thing,* she thought - she poured a glass for herself and then one for Wes before walking to their bedroom. She deftly closed the door behind her using a combination of her left foot and her backside to make sure it was closed.

Kristin stared at Wes on the bed as he read today's newspaper, his right foot boosted up on a couple of pillows. She loved watching him do even a simple thing like this, and warmth filled her heart as she considered just how well her life played out right now.

Kristin strode over to Wes' side of the bed and sat down next to him at his hip.

"I thought you might like this," she told him, as she offered him the cold glass.

Wes folded down the newspaper and tossed it onto the floor beside the bed.

"Thanks," he said with a sigh and a smile. Just the feel of Kristin's body next to his put Wes more at ease than he had felt for the day, especially since the injury.

Kristin reached in with her wine glass and clinked it on Wes' before each of them took a sip. The combination of the cold and dry of the wine, along with the sweet notes, gave Kristin just the warmth she hoped for. Kristin watched as Wes sipped his wine and then looked up. Kristin reached over to grasp his glass and put both glasses down on his nightstand before she leaned her body close to his.

Kristin kissed Wes deeply and pressed her breasts against Wes' chest as she did. Her right hand grazed the stubble on his cheek, and she felt the familiar grip of his hands at her hips as Wes held her close. Kristin slowly pulled her lips back from his and offered up a sly smile. She knew that she wanted more than just kissing tonight.

Her hands moved down over Wes' muscular chest, and she could feel his heart beating strongly through his t-shirt. She quickly put her hands on either side of Wes and pulled herself on top of him so that she straddled him now. Kristin looked down at him and gave another grin as her fingers skillfully worked the buttons of her blouse until her shirt was open. She tossed the shirt aside, leaving herself in her favorite white lacy bra. She pulled Wes' t-shirt over his head so she could run her fingers over his taut pecs.

Their kissing intensified, and the movements became more frenetic as each reached for the other. Hands roamed over each other's chest and torso, and Wes' arousal made its presence known to both. Kristin eagerly pulled off her trousers while never leaving the bed, and she tugged at the sweatpants Wes wore. When she stood at the bottom of the bed and started to pull the pants over Wes' ankles and feet, Wes cried out in obvious pain. Startled, Kristin stopped her actions.

"What's wrong?" she asked with genuine concern.

Wes sat up on the bed and grimaced while he tried to pull his right leg up. When he did this and Kristin finished the removal of his sweats, Wes speedily reached for his ankle. Before he got his hands there, Kristin spied the upper reaches of the bruise above Wes' ankle. She pushed his hands aside and pulled his sock down a bit more, causing Wes' significant discomfort and a brief groan through gritted teeth, so she could see the black and dark blue that covered his ankle.

"Oh my God, are you okay? What happened?"

"It looks worse than it is Kris, really," Wes answered as he tried to grab his sock to cover the bruise. Kristin adamantly defied Wes' efforts and pulled the sock off his foot to examine the rest of the injury.

"Wes, this seems pretty bad," Kristin fretted. "We should go to the ER and get it looked at. There could be something broken."

"Dr. Emerson already looked at it," Wes told her. "He thinks it's just a bruise. I just have to be careful for a few days, ice it, and I'll be fine."

"You don't sound or look fine," Kristin said. Her glances shot back and forth from his ankle to his face. "How did you do this? Jumping off the roof?"

"Very funny," Wes said, without an appreciation for the sarcasm. "I hurt it in the backyard." Wes hoped he could just leave it at that without going into too much detail, but he knew Kristin's persistence wasn't likely to keep from her asking more.

"Where in the backyard? What were you trying to do back there? It's nothing but ice and snow right now."

"Come here," Wes said. He patted Kristin's usual side of the bed so she could come and sit next to him and stop staring at or touching his sore foot.

Kristin slid onto the bed, and Wes put his arm around her, so her head rested on his shoulder.

"I… I went up to the batting cage today," Wes said with hesitation.

"You haven't been up there in months," she softly replied. Kristin put the pieces together before Wes even finished explaining what had happened.

"I was just going up to check on things at first." Wes knew this stretched the truth a bit. "I looked around, and then I just wanted to take a few swings. I was rusty, of course, and fouled one off on my ankle. It got me pretty good. After that, I slipped coming back down the hill and made it worse."

Kristin lay quietly on Wes' shoulder for a moment.

"So, how was it?" Kristin stated gently.

"How was what?"

"Taking swings," she said. Kristin lifted her head off his shoulder and sat up. "I'm not naïve, Wes. I know what time of year it is and how you might feel right now, not being in Florida. Of course, you miss it. It was your life for so long. So how was it?"

Wes didn't know how he should answer. He didn't want to lie to her; he never did. He also didn't want her to worry or feel hurt because he tried to hide something from her, even though he was in a way.

"It felt good," he admitted. "I hadn't realized how much I did miss baseball until today. It took a little bit, but after a while, it came back easily, and I was… I was in a good groove."

"You kept going even after you hurt your ankle?"

"Yes," Wes answered before he gazed over at her. Kristin looked down and away from him briefly, unsure just what to think.

"Are… are you going to go back up there to hit more?"

"Well, not tomorrow or anything. Not with my ankle like this. But when it's feeling better, I think I will. Does that bother you?"

Now it was Kristin's who felt uncomfortable about answering. Kristin scooted down to the bottom of the bed and rose. She walked over to her dresser, looked at herself in the mirror, and saw Wes' reflection behind her as he lay on the bed. She reached behind her back and unclasped her bra, removed it, and tossed it onto the top of her dresser before she stretched into the top drawer to pull out a gray nightshirt.

"Kris?" Wes' stated as he waited for her to answer.

Kristin pulled the nightshirt over her head and tugged it on. She inhaled deeply before saying anything.

"Wes, if that is what you want to do, you should do it. It will make you feel better." She looked into the mirror the whole time and never turned to face him. She tossed her hair, so it was outside of the nightshirt and beheld her eyes in the mirror. She wished nothing presented there that might give away how she really felt before she turned around. "I know something has been bothering you for the last week or so. This can be a good outlet for you."

"You still didn't answer me," Wes said with a bit more concern in his voice now. "Does it bother you?"

"No, it doesn't," Kristin answered, pushing her lips into a smile.

"Good," Wes nodded, feeling relieved. He smiled broadly at her and opened his arms. "You should come back to bed," he offered, pulling the duvet cover and blanket down.

"I'm going to get some ice for that ugly thing on your ankle," she told him as she gently replaced the pillow that was under his foot and lifted his foot onto it.

"Oh man," Wes said with disappointment.

"Your loss, Mr. Martin," she said as she flipped up the hem of her nightshirt, revealing her white panties, as she walked out of the bedroom and into the kitchen.

Kristin stood before the refrigerator for a moment before she pulled open the freezer drawer. She reached in and pulled one of the ice wraps that laid on top of the ice. One was still not frozen yet, and it gave away that he used it all day, probably even when they talked on the phone earlier.

She picked up another, firmer wrap and slowly shut the freezer door. She saw her dim, shadowy reflection in the stainless steel of the fridge. Kristin took some deep breaths to steady herself before she went back into the bedroom.

She hadn't the chance to even talk about her day, about how Karen and Brian got engaged, how great it made her feel to help Izzy out the way she had, or anything else on her mind. All of that abruptly placed itself on the back burner.

"Kris, you coming back?" she heard Wes yell from the bedroom.

"On my way," her voice cracked slightly as she gripped the ice wrap tighter.

5

The pain lingered in Wes' ankle much longer than he thought it would or wanted it to. Each morning he got out of bed anticipating that it would feel better, only to be disappointed when he put weight on it or turned a certain way, and the familiar sting returned that forced him to sit down. Wes even took the time to go down to Dr. Emerson's office to have it examined again and have x-rays taken, but the tests came back showing nothing more than a deep bone bruise. Wes knew of players that suffered an injury like this while he played, and in some cases, it could lay a ballplayer up for a month or more as it healed.

Every day that went by where things weren't better meant one more day that he couldn't swing, get in better shape, or even try to latch on with another team. Teams wouldn't look for a guy who sat out most of last season under the best of circumstances, but spring training moved on, and that window was steadily closing on Wes.

Hiding disappointment became more difficult as days dragged into two weeks, and two weeks turned to three. Wes' frustration built, and the last thing he wanted to do was take it out on Kristin or Izzy, but he found himself with a much shorter fuse than ever before. It just took the sight of some of Izzy's things on the floor in the living room for him to finally blow up.

"Isabelle!" Wes bellowed as he kicked the pile of clothes with his left foot, so he didn't hurt his right more.

Izzy slowly made her way down each step of the staircase. She knew from her father's tone of voice and his use of her full first name that she wasn't being called for a good reason.

"What's up, Dad?" she said as she took a deep breath.

"How many times do you have to be told about leaving your stuff on the floor? There are clothes all over the place." Wes kicked the clothing out a bit further so that the shirts and pants all spread across the floor.

"They weren't all over the place until you kicked them," Izzy mumbled as she plodded down the steps to pick up her things.

"What was that?" Wes snapped.

"Nothing, Dad," Izzy huffed. She squatted down to pick up her clothes and put them back into a pile to bring them upstairs.

Once she had pulled them together, Izzy rose and stood face to face with her father. She and Kristin spoke days ago about Wes, how he acted lately, and how they needed to keep trying to smooth things over as he dealt with this tough experience in his life. Izzy tried to rise to the challenge, but incidents like this became more and more frequent and started to frazzle her already anxious teenage nerves.

"Anything else?" Izzy remarked, trying not to sound too sarcastic, even though she wanted to so badly.

"Yes, the kitchen garbage needs to go out. If you could do that, I would appreciate it," Wes answered as he worked to regain some composure.

"Fine." Izzy walked up the stairs, stomping on each step a bit harder than usual to vent her frustration.

"No need to stomp!" Wes yelled. "And you better not just toss that pile of clothes on the floor in your room. That place is a mess as it is."

Izzy rolled her eyes and mimicked Wes as she walked towards the door to her room. Kristin had just opened the bathroom door in the hall and almost ran right into Izzy as she passed. Kristin knew by the way Izzy moved that something else was wrong.

"What's the matter?" Kristin asked. Izzy waved to Kristin for her to follow her as she went into her room. Kristin made her way down the hall and shut the bedroom door behind her.

"I get Dad is going through a tough time right now, but I don't know how much more of this I can take," Izzy said. She tossed the clothing she held onto the top of her dresser before she sat down on her bed. "He takes every little thing out on me."

Kristin sat down next to Izzy.

"Izzy, I know it's been hard for you, and he's been rough to deal with. Hopefully, he will start feeling better…"

"Kris," Izzy interrupted. "We've said that for weeks now, and he's not feeling better. He just gets grumpier every day. He doesn't even get changed out of his sweats most days. I tried to get him to drive me to school or even just go down to Grandma and Grandpa's to visit, and he won't do that. He just stays cooped up in the house, staring out the back windows. We need to do something."

Kristin sighed. "I don't know what I can do, Izzy. He doesn't even want to talk to me about it. Anytime I bring up baseball or his ankle or anything like it, he just stares at me and nods, like he's not really listening."

"Well I'll be glad to talk to him about it," Izzy said as she got up from the bed and moved towards the door.

"I don't think that's the answer either," Kristin said. She grabbed hold of Izzy's wrist before she could turn the doorknob. Kristin then reached and gave Izzy a hug from behind, holding her.

"I'll talk to him, I promise. Try not to overthink it. Concentrate on other things instead. What's going on with the musical?"

"They announce the cast this week," Izzy said as she pressed her back into Kristin, letting herself get hugged tighter. "I really hope I get Ariel."

"I know you'll get it," Kristin reassured her. "You have a great voice, the smile, and let's not forget this red hair." Kristin took some of Izzy's red locks into her hand and held it up while smiling.

"Thanks, Kris," Izzy replied. Izzy went and sat down at her desk and flipped open the lid to her laptop. "I've got some homework to finish."

"Homework to finish or Bradley to talk to?" Kristin said with a smirk.

"Maybe a little of both," Izzy said coyly.

"Okay, but don't make it too long with Bradley. If your father hears you and comes in here, you know he will explode. And maybe clean up a little bit in here, please?"

"I promise." Izzy made a cross with her index finger over her heart.

Kristin exited the bedroom and made her way down the hall towards the stairs. She walked down quietly, listening to try to hear what room Wes might be in. She had hoped he went downstairs to the entertainment area, a place he rarely frequented lately.

She got to the living room and found all the lights out, and the only light on in the kitchen was the one they routinely left on over the sink. Kristin saw the lights on in the bedroom, which meant Wes already holed himself up in there again.

Kristin stood in the doorway to the bedroom for a moment, eyeing Wes as he laid on the bed. He wore his pajama bottoms and t-shirt already, even though the time showed barely past eight at night. He also propped his foot upon the pillow already with the familiar ice wrap on it.

Kristin walked over and stood at the foot of the bed.

"Want to go out to the diner and grab some dessert? I know they have banana cream pie today, your favorite."

Wes glanced up from reading the newspaper, the sports section naturally, and looked at Kristin.

"I'm not really hungry," he answered, going back to reading the paper.

"Okay, well how about we just go down to your parents and see them? I haven't been down there with you in weeks. I'm sure your Mom and Dad would love to see you. I have a couple of books I wanted to give Jenny anyway."

Kristin waited patiently for Wes to answer.

"I don't know," Wes told her. "Why don't you just run down and drop the books off? Mom would love to chat with you."

"Well how about we go downstairs, cuddle on the couch and watch a movie?" Kristin did her best to mask her growing frustration.

"I don't think there's anything I really want to watch," Wes stated, folding the newspaper and moving to the next page.

Kristin marched over towards Wes and grabbed the newspaper from his hands before tossing it across the room.

"Alright Wes, I've tried to be nice and accommodating with you. I get that you're frustrated, upset, sad, or even a little depressed right now, I really do, but we can't just spend every night going to bed at eight with you brooding about things. It's affecting you, it's affecting Izzy, and it's affecting me."

"How is it affecting you and Izzy?" Wes answered. "I'm just keeping to myself and trying to work through this. I just want my ankle to feel better."

"Wes, it's getting to all of us." Kristin sat next to Wes on the bed and took his left hand in hers. "Seeing you like this every day is eating me up. I want to help you, but you won't let me in to do that. And you constantly ride Izzy about anything and everything. You were never like that. We need to do something."

"What do you want me to do, Kris?" Wes raised his voice. "Time is passing by, and all I can do is sit around and watch it happen. We're at the end of February, and I haven't been able to do what I want. I just want to feel better so I can get back up there and hit and maybe…" Wes let his voice trail off.

"And maybe what? Do you want to try to play again?"

"Maybe I do," Wes said quietly.

Kristin sat quietly for a moment. In the back of her mind, she thought that this was where everything would lead.

"Why didn't you say something about this to me weeks ago? Did you think I wouldn't support you? Wes, you have to know that I would be there for you no matter what you decided to do. You need to be honest and open with me. I thought we were a team here, the three of us."

"I don't know why I didn't say anything about it, Kris," Wes confessed. "I think part of me knew I wanted to at least try to go back, to see what I could do. I feel like, I don't know that I left things unfinished and that I still have that passion for playing. I guess I was a little embarrassed about it, too."

"You don't have to feel embarrassed about something you have passion for." Kristin gripped Wes' hand tighter. "Wes, I don't want you to just give up on anything you aren't ready for. Don't do that. I would hate to think you didn't try and then… then you might resent me like I was the reason you stopped playing."

"I never said that, and I never felt that way." Wes sat up, moved closer to Kristin, and looked her in the eyes.

"I know you never said it, Wes, but the way you walked away from the game last year to come back home, I guess part of me always worried that you might have quit and never got the chance to finish last year the way you wanted to."

"Kris, I did finish last year the way I wanted to… right here with you and Izzy. When I walked away from Cincinnati last year, it was the right thing for me to do. I needed to do that for me. Maybe this is just a passing feeling, and once I try it, I won't want to do it, but I know that I have to find that out. The more time I have to sit here and think about it, the more I know that's true. I'm sorry I have been so hard on you and

Izzy. It's been beyond frustrating to me, and there were many times I wanted to share that with you, I just couldn't bring myself to do it. For that, I'm sorry too."

Kristin sniffled back some tears coming and leaned in and kissed Wes, softly at first and then with more feeling.

"I love you, Wes," Kristin told him. "Don't shut me out or feel like you have to hide things from me. Good or bad, you need to talk to me, okay?"

"I promise," Wes said, making the crossing motion over his heart, which caused Kristin to giggle. "And you have to promise to not hide things from me, like telling me when I am an asshole, or anything else."

Kristin paused for a moment and then broke into a smile.

"Oh, don't worry. If I don't, I am sure Izzy will be glad to."

Wes grabbed Kristin and rolled her onto the mattress, causing her to squeal with laughter.

6

Wes awoke to sunshine that streamed through the gap in the curtains, a gap just large enough to let the morning rays dance across his face. He squinted and turned to his alarm clock and saw it was already passed nine, causing him to sit up quickly. Wes let the morning slip away again, and Kristin and Izzy were long gone to work and school, meaning he missed them once again. With the way his mood swung lately, there were good mornings and bad ones. Sometimes he just stayed in bed, staring at the ceiling as he wondered if his ankle might ever heal fully or if his baseball life had just passed him by.

This morning Wes got out of bed and walked to the bathroom, his only thought about that it was late and he should get his day started. Not until after he brushed his teeth and stepped on his way back towards the bedroom, did he experience the realization that he walked without any pain. Wes stopped and stared down at his feet. At first, he wiggled his toes, and gingerly moved his right foot up and down off the ground. Everything felt good for the first time in weeks. A grin swept across Wes' face as he put more weight on his ankle and shifted his feet back and forth. He could move without even the slightest twinge of discomfort.

Wes didn't think twice about what his next move would be. He stripped out of his pajamas quickly and put on a t-shirt and sweatpants. He sat down to put on his socks and sneakers and looked closely at the right ankle that gave him so much trouble over the last several weeks. The bruise that marked his ankle was faded and almost gone, finally. Wes finished getting dressed, grabbed a sweatshirt from the closet, and headed towards the back door.

Wes was a bit leery about making his way back to the batting cages. He peered outside and saw the bright sun, but there were still some hints of melting ice that dotted the yard all the way up to the building in the back. He grabbed the wooden cane in the corner that his father had brought up for him a few weeks ago while he healed and decided to bring it along, just to keep things safe in case he should run into trouble.

The first step onto the back lawn saw his sneaker sink a bit into the softening grass. The temperature had risen quite a bit lately, a warm spell in March for Western Pennsylvania, which started to make Wes even antsier to swing again. Wes took small steps and tried to stay safe, and even walked the long way around up to the back to avoid more significant swaths of ice that lingered on the lawn. When he made it up to the building successfully, he looked back down towards the house. Wes smiled and felt accomplished before he unlocked the door and stepped inside.

Wes didn't waste any time today. He turned everything on quickly, grabbed a bat and a helmet, and got in the cage right away. He set the pitching machine to just do fastballs for now, and eagerly awaited the first one coming in at him. His fingers tightened around the bat, and when the first pitch came in, Wes took a soft swing at it, afraid to test his ankle too much right away. He sent a slow chopper off to the left, and it dribbled aside, but Wes nodded in approval of it. The critical part of the process was nothing hurt.

Wes spent the next forty-five minutes swinging, mixing up the pitches, and making good contact most of the time. He finished the session with a flourish as he smacked a line drive so it rattled off the back netting. Wes gave the bat a toss in a way he never did when he played and smiled triumphantly. He walked out of the batting cage, grabbed a towel, and wiped the sweat from his head and arms. Wes sat back on the chair in front of the computer that charted his sessions and saw he had contacted over 80% of the pitches, and the connection was mostly solid. He couldn't have asked for anything better.

Wes left the back building and followed the same easier route down to the house that he took going up. He heard the snow and ice rapidly melt on the trees nearby, and he got to the patio and yelled, "Yes!" loudly enough that it echoed. Once inside, Wes went to the fridge and grabbed a bottle of water, first pressing it against his forehead to help him cool down a bit, before he twisted off the cap and took a long draw on the bottle. Wes wanted to share his excitement with someone, and he picked up his cell phone to call Kristin at the library. He tried her line, but it went right to voicemail.

"Hey Kris," he said happily. "Sorry I missed you leaving this morning. Give me a call when you get the chance. It's nothing terrible, I promise."

Wes ended the call and thought about who he could contact next when he realized he didn't have any other friends nearby to call and tell about his victory. It bothered him a little, to be distanced from the people he considered his friends, but the truth was that they were all ballplayers who were either at spring training in Arizona or Florida or guys who had retired and lived further away.

Wes returned to the bedroom, stripped out of his sweaty clothes, and went to get in the shower. As he washed and allowed the water to take the dried sweat away, he realized who his next call needed to be to, but he was unsure how it would go. He hadn't spoken to his agent, Randy, in months, since Wes passed on that commentator job one of the networks wanted him to take. Randy wasn't happy with the decision, and even though they exchanged Christmas cards, the two hadn't talked since the disagreement.

Wes spent the whole time in the shower trying to go over in his head what he would say to Randy, how to smooth things over, and how to approach the idea of maybe getting a tryout with someone. He sat on his bed, wrapped in a towel, and stared at his cell phone the whole time with Randy's number pulled up.

****

Kristin had been locked into a meeting all morning with the library's board, going over business updates, the budget, and other details. She spent the last week or so readying for the meeting so that she had access to the information the board might ask for, and Kristin even prepared for some of the questions she knew they were bound to ask. The programs she introduced over the last year brought more people to the library than ever before, including many that lived beyond Chandler but liked all the library now had to offer. The speakers, classes, and more she arranged produced more visitors to the library and the town in general, and she worked hard to generate positive word of mouth, feedback, and business not just for the library but the other places in town.

As Kristin sat through the meeting, she found her mind wandered, as it had been wont to do lately. Even though she and Wes talked a lot about what he dealt with right now, and she tried to be as supportive as possible, part of her still worried about how it would all play out. Kristin always saw herself as a strong, independent, and assertive woman, but she some insecurities lingered when it came to her relationship with Wes. Kristin loved him dearly, and she knew he felt the same way about her, but she also knew that his pro career worked as a powerful draw for him. Competing with the feelings he had about baseball she thought was something long gone, but with the recent revelations about Wes' desire to play again, she didn't know what to think.

Kristin stared out the window and watched the water droplets from the melting icicles on the eaves patter down onto the windowsill. The ice and snow thawed more each day, and the weather warmed, with hints of the spring to come more prevalent all the time. She knew the warm weather made the itch Wes felt even stronger, and part of her was almost grateful for the ankle injury that held him up from practicing more. Maybe the spring would come, Wes' ankle still wouldn't be fully healed, and he might give up on the thoughts of playing again and move on. Kristin realized these were selfish thoughts, but the idea crept into her mind more and more lately.

"What do you think, Kristin?" Pauline Scott, one of the board members, asked her.

"Hmmm? I'm sorry, I got lost for a minute. Think about what?"

"I know it's easy to start getting spring fever with the weather lately, but we really need you to focus," Pauline chastised.

Even after all the hard work she put in, Kristin still got a hard time from many of the board members, an older contingent reluctant to a lot of the changes she had implemented and always wanted to do.

Kristin took a deep breath and mentally counted to five to calm her nerves. She then gave a genteel smile to Pauline.

"You're right, Pauline. My apologies. Can you ask your question again, please?"

"I was wondering if that expense for upgrading the Wi-Fi in the library is essential. We already offer Internet access. Do we need it to be that much better for people coming in? It seems like a lot of money."

"It's an investment," Kristin explained. "Young people are less likely to come to us to do work, research, or look for books and information if they know we have lousy Internet access. They are the patrons we are trying to bring in more so they can see all we have to offer and use our services. Besides, we only have a few computers, and patrons are always waiting to use them. If people could bring their own laptops and use them, it would be better for all of us. I got three price quotes for the work, and the one Jim Gentry quoted us was the best of them."

"I think we need to look into this more," Pauline retorted, straightening her glasses on her pointy nose.

Kristin looked at the other members of the board, all of whom were forty or fifty years older than her. It became more challenging to convince them of modernizing the rest of the library assets as she wanted after getting so much out of them last year. Kristin had used Wes to her advantage last year, with the board members enamored of her relationship with him and that she routinely brought him to parties and fundraisers. This year she determined to take on tasks on her own, to show the members that she was the driving force behind the ideas that helped to make the library better. If she just had one ally on the board that she could count on and who looked at her as more than Wes Martin's girlfriend, Kristin knew she could make some headway.

"Okay, let's table that idea for now," Marion Harris, the director of the library and the one who hired Kristin a year ago, stated, wanting to move the meeting forward.

"We shouldn't wait too long," Kristin stated to Marion and the others on the board. "Spring is coming, kids will be writing research and term papers, and we are going to need it before the school year ends. It might take a week or so to get the work done, and I don't know if Jim will be available to start right away if we hold off on things."

"I'm sure it will be fine," Pauline added, cutting Kristin off.

"Now, on to the Spring fundraiser dinner. We can do the same as last year and have the dinner at Angelo's," Marion stated. "I already talked to Angelo about it, and he's willing to give us the whole restaurant for the night. We can work on the menu and figure out how much to charge per person. Kristin, I hope Wes will be joining us again this year?"

Kristin held back her sigh. "I'll have to ask him to make sure he is free," she said politely.

"Oh, I'm sure he will be," Fred Clark, another board member and owner of the local barbershop, chimed in. "He's retired. What else will he have to do?" he chuckled. The rest of the board members laughed and nodded in agreement.

"I know he's retired, Fred," Kristin said as she gripped the arm of her chair. "But he does have things of his own to do, too. I don't know if he's made other commitments, is working on the farm, helping with Jenny, or what. I will ask him."

"Well, having him there helped us sell out the dinner last year," Fred added. "I don't know if we can do that without him, and he worked to secure a lot of donations. Maybe you can, you know, convince him, to go," Fred said with a wink.

"Excuse me?" Kristin roared. "That's utterly inappropriate of you to suggest, Fred."

Kristin stood up and began to gather her things. The board members looked on, flabbergasted.

"I'm sure Fred was just making a joke," Marion said, as she glared at Fred. "As in bad taste as it was, he surely didn't mean it, did you, Fred?"

Fred, now with all eyes on him, should have known better to feel the pressure and to try to backtrack on his statements. Instead, he opted to double down.

"All I'm saying is that a pretty girl like Kristin could use her… you know… assets, to make him see that it's a good idea to go."

Marion rolled her eyes and groaned. Kristin slammed her paperwork into her bag. She knew if she stayed in that room a minute longer, she was going to leap across the table and leave the town minus a barber and a barbershop.

"It's time for me to get back to work," Kristin huffed. She grabbed her things and stormed out of the meeting room they used in the town hall. Kristin's heels clacked loudly on each step she hit, and she whisked herself out of the building and into the sunlit street, grateful for the light breeze that blew because it might help cool her down.

Kristin muttered to herself the entire two-block walk to the library, and more than one person turned to look at her as she marched along talking to no one. When she reached the library, she flung open the doors so that they clapped loudly when they shut, causing people in the library to turn their heads. The noise grabbed the attention of Karen right away, who was positioned at the front desk.

Karen watched as Kristin chugged by her and into her office and slammed the door behind her, so it rattled the glass pane. Karen glanced around the library as people stared before she broke out in a smile.

"Next show is in thirty minutes, folks," she said. "Stick around and see what happens next!"

Karen slipped into Kristin's office and closed the door quietly. Kristin sat at her desk, viciously typing on her keyboard.

"Geez, Kris, what's wrong? You came in here like Jerome Bettis running through the line."

Kristin looked up from her keyboard, her face red, and her eyes peering like Clint Eastwood.

"What?" Kristin answered, sounding angry and confused at the same time.

"Pittsburgh football reference," Karen said. "Never mind. It took enough to get you to understand baseball. What happened?"

"The monthly board meeting happened is what, and Fred Clark is a Dark Ages moron. He basically told me to go home and have sex with Wes to convince him to come to this year's fundraising dinner so the library would make more money. Nice to know that the board thinks it's okay to just pimp me out like that."

Karen sat down in the chair across from Kristin.

"Sadly, that sounds just like Fred," Karen told her. "I can only imagine the locker room talk that goes on in that barbershop. Did anyone say anything to him?"

"Marion tried to give him an out, but he just dug himself in deeper to make things more offensive. I am so tempted to just turn in my resignation right now."

"No way!" Karen yelled. "You are not leaving me here by myself. Besides, you're the best thing to happen to this library in forever. Without you, who knows how bad things would get in here. Just give yourself a few minutes to calm down. Want some coffee? How about I run out and get us some cashew chicken from Tiger Palace?"

"Ugh, I can't even think about eating right now," Kristin said, her face looking sour suddenly.

"Okay, well, don't do anything rash," Karen begged. "We need you here, Kris. I need you here. Who's going to help me plan the wedding if you're not in here every day?"

"Don't worry, I'll be fine," Kristin answered gruffly, waving her hand to get Karen out the door.

Once Karen left, Kristin went back to her computer. The thought of a resignation letter was real to her for a passing moment, but she could never go through with it. Even so, she wanted to let Marion know how she felt about the meeting. She started to write an email, and while she read things over, she remembered to turn her phone back on after she shut it off before the meeting. Her phone came to life and dinged, letting her know she had a missed call and a message. Kristin saw it was from Wes and listened.

Wes sounded more upbeat than he had in days. She wondered what happened to put him in such a good mood. Kristin was grateful for whatever it could be, but when she tried to call him back, several unanswered rings occurred before it went to voicemail.

"Tag, you're it," Kristin said, as she tried to hide her own feelings of frustration from the day.

I'm glad one of us is having a good day, she thought. Kristin put her hand down on her stomach as it grumbled some more.

7

Nervousness overcame Wes as he picked up his cell phone and pressed the number for his agent, Randy Miller. Randy tried to get Wes to do all kinds of things after the retirement last year, and at the time Wes showed little interest in doing anything beyond spending quality time with Kristin and Izzy. Several times the two of them argued over doing interviews, commercials, and things like that, but Wes almost always won out. A few times he gave in to Randy just so his agent would stop pestering about things, but mostly Wes just went on with his life. Now he worried about how the conversation would go.

Wes got Randy's assistant and calmly asked to speak with Randy, letting the woman know it was Wes Martin. The assistant's voice sounded new, not the Southern accent of Randy's typical assistant Kacey, and Wes knew the woman had no idea who he was or what he might want. He hoped he wouldn't just get put on hold, left there for a bit, and then told Randy was in a meeting, something Randy often did when he got a call from a client or potential client he didn't really want to talk to.

After listening to a few verses of "Hold On" by Wilson Phillips, something Randy thought was hysterical to use for his on-hold music, the phone finally clicked back on.

"Wes Martin," Randy chimed in. "I thought maybe you fell off the earth. How's it going, Wes? Izzy and Kristin doing well?"

"Hey Randy," Wes replied. "Yes, they are both doing well, thanks for asking. Say, where's Kacey? That wasn't her who answered the phone."

"Kacey moved on to greener pastures. She hooked up with one of my football players and left me to go to Oakland. It was a damn shame. She was with me for over ten years. My new assistant, Tammy, is great though. A real sparkplug and she's easy on the eyes too. Anyway, I'm sure that's not why you called me. What's going on? I usually don't hear too much from my retired clients."

Wes breathed deeply and then started in with his pitch.

"Here's the thing Randy. I've been thinking… well, more than thinking. I've been hitting, and it's felt pretty good and going well. I guess it has given me a bit of an itch that I need to scratch. I was wondering… well, I was wondering if you thought there might be any interest in me coming back with someone."

Randy was quiet for a moment, and Wes didn't take this as a positive sign.

"Are you sure about this, Wes? When you left, you felt confident that you were done. Hell, no one walks away from the game with a finish like you had. It came right out of a movie, hitting those home runs and all against the Pirates. With all the other stuff I offered you over the months, I thought you just wanted to be done with baseball."

"I did, Randy," Wes answered. "But… I don't know, I miss it, and I think I still have something left to offer. I've kept myself in pretty good shape, and the bat is there for sure. I'm sure once I started fielding drills, it would all come back quickly. If you could get me a tryout with someone, I know I could…"

"Wes, hold on," Randy said, cutting Wes off before he could go further. "It's already the beginning of March. You've got what, maybe 2 or 3 weeks left in spring training? Latching on with someone this late without having any real time to get into playing shape is a tall order. Most teams are pretty set when it comes to the rosters they think they will have for Opening Day. You'd have to be willing to go to extended spring training, probably spend some time in the minors, and even then, there are no guarantees. You really want to do all of that?"

"I know it might be a long shot, Randy, but I have to try. Can you at least put some feelers out there and let me know what you find?"

"Are you willing to look beyond Pittsburgh? I didn't think you were too keen on doing that. What does Kristin think about all this? Or Izzy?"

"They don't know anything about all of this yet, Randy, and I want to keep it that way. If something came up worth considering, then I will talk to them about it. Until then, it's just between you and me. I'm… I'm willing to go anyplace. Maybe there's an AL team looking for a DH or an NL team that wants a bat off the bench, whatever."

Wes heard Randy's chair creak and a sigh came from Randy.

"Okay, let me see what I can do. I can't make you any promises, Wes. This is a tough one. The baseball landscape is a lot different now. Teams are willing to go with younger guys that cost less and give them more control. There are still guys out there waiting for contracts, and those are guys that played all of last season."

"Thanks, Randy. That's all I'm asking."

"Okay, give me a couple of days to see what I can find. In the meantime, you should talk to Izzy and Kristin about this to make sure they are okay with it too. You walked away for them, remember?"

"I know Randy. Everything feels, well, unfinished, is all. Just let me know what you can find."

"You got it. Talk to you soon," Randy added before hanging up.

A tinge of guilt washed over Wes. He didn't want to come off as being selfish, and that was what Randy implied. Putting his family first had been an important priority for him when he left the game, and Kristin filled a big hole that existed in Wes' life for a long time. He could never forget that. But Wes also knew that if he didn't at least try, at least find out if a team wanted him and if he could still perform, he would always regret it.

The harder part would be telling Kristin and Izzy that this is what he wanted to do now.

****

The workday wouldn't end fast enough for Kristin. She spent the rest of the day annoyed about how things went at the board meeting and how insulting Fred Clark had been to her. Her contributions to the library were much more than having Wes Martin as a boyfriend, and to insinuate anything else made Kristin boil over. She wrote and rewrote an email to Marion four times before she finally sent one that seemed composed and controlled while still getting her point across. Marion had yet to get back to her and the day neared an end, which left Kristin to stew even more.

By the time the last patron left the library, Kristin had packed and anxiously wanted to call it a day. She walked out to the front desk and stood there with her bag over her shoulder, watching Karen pile up the last of the books to be re-shelved in the morning.

"A little eager to leave today?" Karen remarked.

"You know it," Kristin answered coldly.

"I know Fred Clark pissed you off, Kris, but don't let his attitude consume you. He's not worth it," Karen said as she shut off her computer.

"No, he's not worth it, but what he said makes it seem like the only thing I bring to the table here is Wes. It just makes me wonder how many other people involved with the library feel the same way as he does and aren't saying it out loud."

"Hey, people here are aware of what you do, and that has nothing to do with Wes. Unfortunately, we live in a small town where Wes has always been the hero, and some may never see beyond that. If that's the way they want to think, screw them. Don't let that drag you down."

"You're right Karen," Kristin replied, "but it still bothers me."

"Want to go down to the barbershop and write in lipstick on the front window 'Fred is a sexist prick?'" Karen said, as she grabbed a lipstick from her purse and smiled.

Kristin grinned and laughed, the first time she felt good today since she left the house.

"Thanks, Karen, but I need to go pick up Izzy from school. She stayed after to go to the announcement of the cast for the musical. I hope at least one of us had a good day today."

"Okay," Karen answered. Karen twisted her tube of lipstick back down and put it away. "Go ahead, and I'll lock up. I'll be sure to have a good night. Brian and I are getting together to make up a list of potential places for the wedding and talk about who to invite. Can I bring it in tomorrow so we can talk about some stuff?"

"You bet," Kristin smiled. "I'll see you in the morning."

Kristin walked to her car and started it, heading over towards Chandler High School. She had been so caught up in feeling angry about the meeting today that she lost sight of everything else going on in her life. Karen and her wedding, Izzy and the play, Wes' parents, and Wes... what to do about Wes? He never called her back after she left a message, but that didn't necessarily mean anything. He sounded better today, so that was undoubtedly a good sign, and after their talk the night before, she hoped their lines of communication were better now.

Kristin pulled up in front of the school and saw Izzy sitting on a bench. Her boyfriend Bradley sat there with her, his arm around her like he was consoling her.

Oh no, Kristin thought. *Maybe she didn't get the part. Or perhaps he's breaking up with her.*

A dozen things raced through Kristin's head as she stressed over how to deal with Izzy, Wes, her job, and everything else. It was only the knock on the window of the passenger side of her car that broke her trance. Kristin turned quickly and looked to see Izzy, sad-faced, leaning her head against the window. In an instant, however, Izzy cracked into a big grin and slapped a stack of papers on the window. She held the script of the musical, and on the front, it read Isabelle Martin as Ariel.

Kristin unlocked the door and Izzy climbed in, squealing and giving Kristin a big hug.

"You did it!" Kristin yelled. "I am so proud of you. Congratulations! This is awesome!"

"It is awesome!" Izzy rolled down the window and screamed, "This is awesome!!"

"It's excellent news, Izzy. We should celebrate tonight. Let's go home, get your dad, and go out."

"Where are we going to go?" Izzy said. "We only have the diner and Angelo's, and we just had Chinese the other day."

"Maybe we can take a ride up to the mall and go somewhere there."

"I love the sushi place there. Do you think Dad will be up to going out? He hasn't been much for doing anything lately." Izzy looked concerned as they sat in the idling car.

"He sounded better on the phone today," Kristin told her. "Besides, it's a special day for you. I'm sure he will do it. Sushi, huh?" Kristin wasn't thrilled with the choice, but it was Izzy's moment, so she would go along.

"That's okay, right?"

"Of course. You know what, let's really celebrate."

Kristin got out of the car and walked over to the passenger side and opened the door.

"What are you doing?" Izzy said as she watched Kristin.

"You drive. You've had your permit for a week now. Let's get some practice," Kristin told her, pointing at the driver's side.

Izzy had a shocked look on her face, but then quickly slid over behind the wheel so she could drive. Kristin climbed in and sat on the passenger side and made sure to buckle up, and then watched as Izzy put the car in drive and took off.

Izzy started slowly until she reached the edge of the parking lot. She looked cautiously in both directions before gunning the engine so she could turn onto the road and head towards Route 5. Kristin felt the surge of speed as her head pushed back against the headrest.

"Just watch your speed, Izzy," Kristin reminded.

Izzy nodded and moved the car carefully to Martin Way before making the right-hand turn to go to their street.

"Can we invite Grandma and Grandpa too?" Izzy asked Kristin.

"Sure," Kristin nodded.

Izzy made a sharp left turn into the driveway and slammed on the brakes, putting the car into park as Kristin put her hands up on the dashboard.

"I think we need to work on a few things, like speed and braking," Kristin said as she got out of the car quickly.

Izzy raced out of the car and up the front porch into the house. Kristin followed behind at a slower pace and could see Izzy talking to her grandfather when she walked through the door.

"So, we're going to go for sushi to celebrate if you and Grandma want to come with us," Izzy said, talking a mile a minute.

"I think we're going to have to pass tonight, Izzy," Wyatt said to her as he put his arm around Izzy.

"Your grandma isn't feeling too good today. She's in the bedroom laying down."

"Oh, okay," Izzy said, a bit disappointed but understanding. "Is it okay if I go in there and let her know about the musical?"

"Sure, honey," Wyatt told her.

Izzy ran off down the hall to talk to her grandmother, leaving Wyatt and Kristin alone.

"Is Jenny okay?" Kristin said with concern.

"Yeah," Wyatt said, sitting down in his recliner and pointing to the couch to get Kristin to sit as well. "Just one of those bad days, you know. It happens. She just tries to overdo it sometimes; you know how it is."

"All too well," Kristin said with a laugh.

"How is Wes, anyway? I haven't seen him for a few days. Is he actually coming out of hibernation to go out with you tonight?"

"He is, whether he knows it or not," Kristin asserted. "I haven't talked to him all day, but he left me a message today, and he seemed upbeat, so I hope that's a good sign. Sooner or later, Wes is going to start feeling better. I'll make sure he comes down to see you two. There's no excuse for not doing that."

"He's stubborn, like his mother. I'm sure he's avoided me because I don't tell him exactly what he wants to hear. He'll get over it, and even when he does, I'll still give him a hard time. How are you with having to deal with him?"

Kristin sighed.

"I'm holding my own. It's been tough at times, but we had a good talk last night, and I think he's coming around now. I can understand how he feels; I just wish there was something more I could do to help him, and with all the other busy stuff going on lately, I feel like I haven't had much time to spend with him."

"That's relationships for you. It happens in every marriage..." Wyatt realized what he said and cut himself off. "I'm sorry, Kristin. Just a slip of the tongue."

Kristin tried to roll with it and eked out a smile.

"It's okay, Wyatt. I know what you meant by it. I know we act like a married couple all the time, and if that happens at some point, that will be wonderful."

"What do you mean 'if?'" Wyatt barked. "Of course, he's going to marry you. If he doesn't, he's a damn fool, pardon my cussin'. And he's not too old for me to whoop him either."

Kristin laughed loudly. "I appreciate your support, Wyatt."

Izzy came out into the living room and stood in front of Kristin.

"Grandma was thrilled. I'm glad I got to talk to her," Izzy said. "We should go and get Dad."

Kristin rose from the couch, bent down, and gave Wyatt a peck on the cheek. Izzy followed her and did the same thing.

"Wow, you ladies, have made my night. Enjoy your sushi," Wyatt grinned.

Izzy got back behind the wheel, and Kristin got in alongside her.

"Take it slow up the hill, please, Izzy. Your father will kill both of us if you hit his car with mine," Kristin pleaded.

Izzy nodded and moved the car slowly up the hill before bringing it to rest quietly next to her father's. Izzy grabbed her bag off the back seat and ran up the steps to get inside. Kristin could hear her yelling, "Dad!" before she even closed the car door.

Kristin collected her bag and moved slowly up the steps, hearing Izzy clamoring away to Wes in the kitchen.

"We'll have rehearsals after school most days, but I know some of the other kids in the show so I can get rides home, so you and Kristin don't have to come out and get me all the time, at least until I get my license," Izzy said excitedly.

"License?" Wes said, startled. "You've had your permit for a week."

"Kristin let me drive home today, and I did fine, right, Kris?" Izzy asked.

Kristin cracked a smile and gave a thumbs up. "She did fine for the first time on the road."

"See? I can get my license, and then my own car, and you guys won't have to worry about a thing," Izzy stated proudly.

"Now you're getting a car too?" Wes' eyes went wide. "Let's get through dinner tonight and then we can worry about the rest, okay?"

"Fine, Dad," Izzy said with an eye roll. "I'm going up to change my shirt, and then we can go."

Izzy dashed off to change, and Kristin came over and gave Wes a hug.

"Sounds like quite the exciting ride home," Wes said, holding Kristin.

"Exciting is one way to put it. Hey, you're walking around without your cane today," Kristin noticed.

"I know. The ankle feels fantastic today. I went up and did some hitting and exercise. It was great. I feel exhilarated."

Wes bent down and gave Kristin a deep kiss, pulling her into him.

"Let me go grab my wallet and keys so we can get ready to go," Wes said as they broke their kiss.

Kristin watched as Wes walked into the bedroom without a limp or any trouble at all.

Seems like everyone is taking two steps forward today… except me, Kristin told herself.

8

A crowded mall on a Friday wasn't the ideal place for either Wes or Kristin, but they both knew that it made Izzy happy to go out and celebrate her accomplishment. Izzy worked hard to gain her spot in the musical and letting her know it was a meaningful moment for the family mattered. Wes and Kristin, however, both faced distractions, caught up in their own thoughts as the three of them ate their dinner at The Emperor's Palace, the nearest restaurant for sushi. The restaurant featured all the tacky embellishments that one would expect to find in a Japanese place in a mall, but the food never failed their expectations as outstanding.

While Izzy filled up her order with all kinds of sushi and sashimi, Wes kept his choices simple, going with a couple of the rolls he always favored and nothing more. Both Izzy and Wes were surprised when Kristin opted to go for the negimaki instead of having any sushi at all.

"No sushi tonight?" Wes commented, arching an eyebrow.

"No, I feel like trying something different tonight," Kristin said quickly. "It always looks good on the menu, so I figured why not?"

Wes shrugged and nodded, not thinking any else of it. The dinner went on with Izzy talking all about the play, the cast, and what the plans existed for rehearsals, costumes, and more.

"Did Bradley get a part?" Kristin asked as she took a spoonful of the miso soup that served as a first course.

Izzy's face contorted a bit.

"No, he didn't," she pouted. "He had tried out for Prince Eric, but once he found out that the part had singing involved, he didn't want to do it anymore. I complained to him about it, but I didn't get very far. In the end, Justin Madlock got the part of Eric. He's a senior who's done other musicals in the past. He's really good. I think we'll be perfect together."

"Sounds like everything is well planned out. I'm sure between your Dad and I, we can make sure you get all the rides you might need, right, Wes?" Kristin added.

Wes busily poked gently at his salad more than ate it, and the forkful of lettuce and cucumber he held in front of him kept dripping the thick ginger dressing back down into the bowl before some of it hit the table.

"Dad? Are you listening?" Izzy said. She waved her hand in front of her father to get his attention.

"Sorry," Wes answered, "I guess I zoned out. What was the question?"

"About giving me rides to rehearsals," Izzy repeated.

"Sure, I should be able to help out with that. Of course." Wes went back to poking at his salad before the waitress returned to the table carrying all the dinners with her. She quickly placed plates where they belonged and whisked away soup and salad bowls so that everyone could enjoy their meals.

Izzy dove right in and started dunking pieces of sushi into a mix of soy sauce and wasabi, while Wes picked up a bit of dragon roll and ate it. He watched Kristin as he ate, and wondered when he might have the right time to tell her about his phone conversation with Randy today. Kristin took small bites of her beef, barely nibbling at it.

"Your beef okay?" Wes asked her. "You don't seem to be that into it."

"No, it's fine," Kristin replied, putting down her chopsticks. "It's just a lot more than I thought it would be. I'm sure I'll end up taking some home."

"Great!" Izzy said over a mouthful of salmon. "I love the leftovers from here."

When dinner finished, and Kristin's leftovers had been boxed up, Wes, Kristin, and Izzy all waded out into the sea of people at the mall. Since Wes' retirement, he did find it easier to go out in public more without getting instantly recognized by people in the Pittsburgh area, so he moved freely among the crowd and took Kristin's hand in his as they walked along.

Izzy stopped in front of one of the clothing stores, looked in the window and then she turned to Wes and Kristin.

"Hey, some of my friends from school are in there. Is it okay if I go in and hang out with them for a little bit?"

"I don't know, Izzy," Wes said. "It's been a long day for Kristin; she probably wants to get home," Wes said. He hoped Kristin did feel that way, so they didn't have to stay at the mall all night.

Izzy turned her pleading eyes to Kristin, and Kristin gave her a smile.

"It's fine with me," Kristin told Wes. "Let her have time with her friends."

"Okay," Wes relented. "But leave your phone on. When I call, you answer, got it?"

"Thanks, Dad!" Izzy shouted before she ran off into the store.

Wes and Kristin continued walking along, engaging in minimal conversation. They stopped to browse and window shop in a few places, but without any real interest in what they looked at. Neither one seemed to be able to come up with just what to say.

As they moved through the mall, Kristin heard a familiar voice yell from behind. She turned quickly and saw Karen there, smiling.

"What are you guys doing here?" Karen said with surprise.

"Izzy wanted to celebrate getting the lead in the musical, so we came down for dinner. She went off with her friends, so we're just walking around, taking in the sights."

"Well, why don't you guys come with me?" Karen offered. "I'm meeting Brian at the restaurant for drinks. He's getting off work early. We can sit and relax for a bit."

Kristin looked over at Wes to see if he wanted to go. Kristin knew Wes usually wished to opt-out of things like this, so she was stunned when he readily agreed to go along. Kristin was somewhat disappointed since she wished for some alone time with Wes to talk about all that went on in her day and find out more about his.

When the group arrived at the casual restaurant Brian worked at, he already stood leaning against the wall out in front waiting for Karen. Brian smiled as soon as he saw Karen coming and gave her a kiss as she came to him.

"Wow, I didn't know you guys were coming," Brian remarked as he greeted Wes and Kristin, shaking Wes' hand.

"I just ran into them on my way over. You don't mind if they join us, do you?" Karen said, fluttering her eyelashes.

"If you guys would rather be alone…" Kristin started, noticing that this might be a way out.

"No, it's fine. It will be nice to hang out with you guys. Come on," Brian insisted.

Brian led the way back into the restaurant, heading over to the bar area where a booth sat empty. Brian nodded towards the bartender and pointed to the booth, and the bartender gave a quick "OK" sign to indicate Brian could have it. A small crowd of people looked on, a bit annoyed that someone had gained preference over them.

"Pays to know someone," Karen said with a laugh as she slid into the booth next to Brian.

A waitress came over and took a drink order for the table. Karen readily ordered a margarita, while Brian and Wes both got draft beers. The waitress turned to Kristin, who politely ordered a ginger ale.

"Ginger ale? Really?" Karen said. "I thought you would want a drink to forget about the day you had."

"Well, I didn't know we would run into you, and one of us has to drive back home," Kristin said, defending her choice.

"What happened today?" Wes asked concernedly.

"It really wasn't that big of a deal," Kristin said, as she tried to gloss over the events of the day.

"No big deal?" Karen said with a raised voice. Karen turned to Wes to tell the story.

"Kris went to the monthly board meeting and got into it with Fred Clark. He told her she needed to get cozy with you to get you to come to the fundraiser dinner this year. She spat nails and wanted to quit over it."

Kristin gave Karen a light kick under the table to get her to shut up.

"What?" Wes turned to Kristin.

"Why didn't you tell me about that? I would have gone down to that barbershop and…"

Kristin cut off Wes.

"That's precisely why I didn't say anything to you yet," Kristin answered, putting her hand on Wes'. "You don't need to go down there fighting an old man like Fred Clark. Besides, I'm capable of dealing with it all myself. I calmed down, and I am taking care of it."

The waitress came back over with the drinks and passed them out to everyone. There was a bit of awkward silence as everyone stared at their drinks before Brian decided to propose a toast.

"Well," Brian said, raising his glass, "Here's a toast to celebrate."

Karen smiled and raised her glass, and Kristin followed suit. Wes sat there, with a confused look.

"What are we celebrating?" Wes asked.

"Our engagement, silly," Karen said, wrapping her arm around Brian. When Karen saw Wes' surprised face, she spoke again. "Kris didn't tell you?"

Wes turned to Kristin and looked at her. Kristin simply gave a weak shrug.

"When did you get engaged?"

"A few weeks ago," Brian said, not catching on about the miscommunication just yet.

"Congratulations," he said, as the four clinked glasses.

After Wes took his initial sip, he turned to Kristin.

"How come you didn't tell me about their engagement? Is there anything else I need to know?" Wes asked her.

"I don't know. You've been caught up in other things. Lately, there never seemed to be a good time to bring up anything. All you wanted to focus on was getting your ankle healed so you could hit again."

Kristin realized maybe she shouldn't have brought up the subject in front of Karen and Brian, but Wes opened the door.

"You've been hitting? That's great," Brian said with a smile as he took a drink. When Kristin and Karen both shot him glares, he pulled back on his smile.

"He's just tried to get into shape and see how it feels," Kristin told the table.

"Actually, it went really well today," Wes replied. "Well enough that I gave Randy a call this afternoon to talk to him."

Wes kept silent as he took a long draw on his beer, drinking more than half in one swig. Karen and Brian both looked confused about the conversation, and Kristin turned to Wes now, with a look of shock and confusion of her own.

"Who's Randy?" Brian whispered to Karen, who quickly elbowed him to keep him quiet.

"You called Randy?" Kristin shook her head. "Why didn't you say anything? What did you call him for?"

Now that it was out there, Wes knew he had to keep talking about it.

"I called him to talk about… about me maybe getting a tryout with a team before spring training ends."

Wes finished what was left of his beer, just as the waitress was going by. Wes held up the empty glass to her and asked if he could get another.

"So, you are going through with it," Kristin nodded, unsure of what or how to feel.

"I tried to call you, Kris, so we could talk about it, but you never called back, and then we came out with Izzy, and I just haven't had the chance until now."

"I see," Kristin said. She sipped her drink, squeezing the glass so tightly it felt like it would break or just slip out of her hands.

Even in a restaurant filled with patrons, the quiet at the booth was deafening. Brian and Karen kept drinking their beverages while Wes went through his second beer before everyone else finished with their first drinks.

The waitress came by and asked if anyone wanted refills. Wes smiled and indicated he wanted another, while the other three at the table looked at him.

"I think Brian and I are going to take off," Karen said, nudging Brian. "He worked a long day today, and we want to go and relax."

"You guys should stay," Wes said. "Maybe you can find out more things that we haven't told each other."

Kristin shot Wes a look and turned back to Karen.

"You want me to stay?" Karen asked quietly.

"No, you guys should go," Kristin said as she arose and hugged Karen.

"I'll call you tomorrow," Karen whispered before she grabbed Brian's hand and towed him out of the booth.

Kristin slid into the opposite side and stared directly at Wes.

"What was all that?" Kristin asked him sternly.

"What? I just thought they might want to stay to celebrate. Besides, it seems to be the only way for me to find out what's going on in your life."

The waitress returned again and put the beer in front of Wes, and he immediately grabbed it and took a big gulp.

"Wes, you need to slow down," Kristin told him. Kristin called out to the waitress to ask for the check.

"I'm fine, Kris, really. Is there anything else you want to let me know about while we're here? Maybe you hit the lottery or are starring in a movie. Do you have another boyfriend on the side you want to tell me about?"

Even though he was a bit drunk, Wes regretted that as soon as it came out of his mouth. He realized by the look on Kristin's face that she was appalled.

Kristin rapidly gathered up her purse and stood up.

"You're drunk, and you're an ass," Kristin scolded. "I'm going to get Izzy to take her home. Take your time to cool off, sober up, have another or whatever, but find a ride home."

Kristin slammed two twenty-dollar bills down on the table and stormed off, out of the restaurant and into the mall.

Wes was too shocked to immediately do anything about it, and by the time he felt prepared to react, Kristin was long gone. Wes sat back and looked at his beer glass, holding it up and swirling around the half that remained. The waitress reappeared with the check and meekly handed it to Wes when she saw he was the only one left.

"Did you want anything else?" the waitress offered, trying to sound perky.

Wes sat back and polished off his beer.

"No, I think I've had enough, thanks," he told her. Wes took the check from her hands before he scanned it quickly. Wes reached into his wallet and pulled out a fifty, and then picked up the two twenties from the table.

"Here you go," he told the girl. "Keep whatever change there is."

"Thank you, sir!" the girl beamed, happy at the big tip.

I've clearly had enough and said too much, Wes thought to himself.

He picked up his cell phone and thought about calling Kristin to apologize, but he knew she the chances of her answering were slim to none. He also saw that he already received a text message from Izzy:

What did you do?

Wes rose from the table and went out into the mall. The heat from the crowd made him uncomfortable and queasy, so he slipped out the exit closest to the restaurant, knowing the car with Kristin and Izzy was likely on its way by now.

The fresh night air revived him a bit, and he slumped onto the stone bench out in front of the entrance, grateful that he hadn't worn a jacket. He stared off into the parking lot and watched the headlights that beamed towards him and off in the distance.

Now what? He wondered.

Wes picked up his cell phone again, saw no new messages from anyone, and then slid his cell phone screen over to where the icon for the ride app hung so he could click on it. His ride would be to him in about ten minutes.

Until then, everything else needed to wait.

9

Naturally, the ride Wes called for showed up later than expected and that left Wes to sit on the bench outside the mall before it finally rolled in. The drinks Wes drank in short order at the bar started to wear off a bit, and a steady, dull ache made its way into his skull when he climbed into the car. With the way his luck ran that night, the driver also recognized him, meaning Wes had little opportunity to close his eyes and rest for the ride home.

The driver was a nice enough older gentleman, but he went on and on about the Pirates, Wes' playing days, how he should play again, and more. He asked a lot of questions that Wes really didn't feel like answering, but he gave the driver short responses and kept his eyes closed, as he begged internally the man would get the hint and just pay attention to the road instead of droning on and on with incessant questions.

When they reached the road that led up to the house, the remarks kept up about the property, the home, and more. Elation and gratefulness washed over Wes as he got out of the vehicle and gave the driver, whose name was Dave, an autograph, but he refused the selfie the driver wanted to take, knowing he looked less than his best at this point.

Wes made his way into the house, and he immediately noticed the silence. A quick glance at his watch showed it was after 11, and Wes knew that both Izzy and Kristin were likely long in bed for the night. He thought about going up to check on Izzy and then figured it best to check on Kristin first. He gently pushed open the bedroom door and held it tight to keep it from creaking so she wouldn't be disturbed.

Part of Wes hoped that Kristin was still awake so he could apologize to her and talk things over, but when he looked in, he saw Kristin snuggled under the blanket right in the middle of the bed. He walked over to the bed cautiously and saw her eyes shut, and she breathed softly as she slept. Instead of disturbing her and moving her over so that he could take his spot on the bed, Wes gave Kristin a quick peck on the forehead and ambled out of the bedroom, closing the door behind him.

Wes walked downstairs to what everyone called 'his room' and flipped on the lights. He kicked off his shoes and took a seat on one of the swivel chairs at the bar while he tossed his keys and wallet on the mahogany bar top. Wes considered a move to behind the bar to grab a beer but thought better of it based on how the night had already gone for him. Instead, he walked behind the bar to the fridge positioned there and grabbed a cold bottle of water. After downing half the bottle to help rehydrate, Wes went over to the large couch and sat down on what would be his bed for the night. Wes grabbed the blanket draped over the back of the sofa and one of the throw pillows and laid down as he tried to make the best of the situation. His thoughts were consumed about how to deal with his behavior so he could make things up to Kristin.

****

When he awoke in the morning, Wes knew right away that he had a terrible night of sleep. He tossed and turned, and almost fell off the couch several times. He lifted his head up and tried to focus on the watch he had left on his wrist. He saw it was after 9 already, which meant that Izzy and Kristin both should be awake. Wes sat up on the sofa and rubbed his temples to massage the ache he felt. The pain, along with the cottonmouth he experienced, gave him the instant reminder about the previous night. Wes had always been able to hold his liquor well but drinking those three beers in about twenty minutes proved too much even for him.

Wes got to his feet and looked at the end of the bar where he had left his keys and wallet. Positioned next to his belongings, he spied a cup of coffee, a bottle of water, some Advil, and some Tums. Wes quickly tossed the Advil into his mouth and chased them down with the water, and then helped himself to a drink of the still-warm, strong coffee. Just that small taste of the coffee seemed to bring Wes back to life a bit and make him feel better. He saw all these items there and took them as a good sign that maybe Kristin forgave him already for his actions, and Wes made his way upstairs, using the railing to help pull himself along.

Wes got upstairs and walked into the kitchen, still sipping his coffee. He hoped Kristin would be in there, but no sign of her existed. He peeked into the bedroom and saw emptiness, with the bed neatly made and the bathroom door wide open. Wes massaged his forehead again, and he went back to the kitchen. He then heard footsteps pounding down the main staircase that made his headache pulse. Within seconds, Izzy walked into the kitchen and gave her father a quick glance.

"Boy, don't you look great," she said sarcastically as she put a few stray dishes in the dishwasher.

"Thanks," Wes answered as he sat down at the kitchen table. "Where's Kristin?"

"She left hours ago," Izzy said to Wes. Izzy walked to him with the pot of coffee and offered to refill his mug.

Wes held the cup steadily on the table while Izzy poured steaming coffee into it. He took a small sip, so the hotter liquid worked through his system to revive him.

"Where did she go? She didn't have to work today."

"I don't know," Izzy said, pouring herself some coffee before she sat at the table opposite her father. "She just said she didn't want to be here when you woke up."

"Great," Wes bemoaned. "Since when do you drink coffee?"

Izzy poured some flavored creamer into her coffee and drank some.

"Dad, I've been drinking coffee for a while. My friends and I go to the coffee place by the school all the time," Izzy told him, feeling more mature as she sipped.

"Okay, well that's a discussion for another time. Right now, I need to get dressed and find Kristin."

Wes got up from the table and started to move towards the bedroom.

"I wouldn't do that, Dad," Izzy stated. "She was still pretty mad about last night. Maybe you just want to give her some time to herself."

"What do you know about last night?" Wes said with dread.

"I know you weren't in the car with us when we drove home. I know Kris told me all about what happened over drinks with Karen and Brian. I know you put your foot in your mouth and Kris got really upset. I don't understand why people drink at all; it just leads to trouble."

Izzy sat back and drank her coffee more while she stared at her father.

"She couldn't have been too mad if she left me stuff downstairs for when I woke up," Wes rationalized hopefully.

"Yeah, that was me that left that stuff. I figured you would need it. Kris woke me up to let me know she was leaving the house. You're welcome."

Wes turned back and sat down in his chair again, and let loose a deep sigh as he massaged his temples again.

"Want to know what I would do?" Izzy said to him.

"Please, oh Wise One, let me know, with all your experience with relationships," Wes answered.

"If you don't want my help, that's fine," Izzy replied, as she stood up and moved over to the sink, rinsing her now-empty coffee mug. "But I might be the only ally you have right now to help you out." Izzy started towards the kitchen doorway to go back to her room.

"Fine," Wes stated loudly. He pushed out the empty chair Izzy sat in with his foot to let her know she should come back. "Tell me what you would do."

Izzy returned and sat and looked earnestly at her father.

"I wouldn't go chasing all over Chandler for her, number one. If you do find her, you're just going to make her angrier by addressing the whole thing in front of other people, like you did last night. Give her a chance to do what she wants to do today, to get a handle on her feelings, and be ready for her when she comes home."

"And then what?" Wes waited in anticipation with the assumption that there had to be more.

"Then you talk to her, Dad," Izzy told him. "You haven't spent time talking to Kris or me in weeks. You just sit there quietly, and no one knows what's going on with you. Tell her what's in your head, what you are feeling and what you are planning. She deserves to know, and so do I for that matter. What you decide affects all of us, you know, not just you."

"I don't want to make her more upset by talking about wanting to play again," Wes said honestly.

"But if that's what's going through your head, she needs to know that, Dad. It's not fair to us for you to keep it all inside and then tell us the day you are leaving that 'Oh, by the way, I'm going to play baseball again. See you in 6 months.' You can't do that to either of us. I'm not eight years old anymore where you can just leave and shuffle me off to Grandma and Grandpa's for the season. We need to talk about these things, as a family, and Kris is a big part of that too… isn't she?"

Wes sensed a tinge of worry in Izzy's voice.

"Of course, she is, Izzy," Wes reassured her. "You two mean the world to me, and I'm sorry if I hurt you. It's just been a tough time for me, I guess, and with all the two of you have going on in your lives, I thought you had enough to worry about."

"I always want to know what's going on with you, Dad. Having you around for the last year has been incredible. We've got the chance to know each other. That doesn't mean I would be against you playing again, but I sure would miss having you around each day to talk to, hang out with, or annoy." Izzy smiled broadly at her Dad.

"Oh, there's plenty of that going on, don't worry," Wes told her, smiling back. "Okay, I will take your advice and wait for her to come home today so we can talk."

Wes moved over and stood in front of Izzy, opening his arms. Izzy rose and gave her father a big hug.

"Okay, advice time is over," Izzy told him. "Now go take a shower. You smell like old beer bottles."

"Thanks," Wes said snidely. Izzy started bounding off to her room again.

"Where are you going?" Wes asked as he watched her.

"A few of the girls from the cast are picking me up at 11. We have rehearsals today, and then we are going to hang out. Besides, I don't want to be here when you two are making up and getting all mushy." Izzy made kissing noises, before laughing and going upstairs, leaving Wes to clean himself up and figure out how he was going to talk to Kristin.

****

Kristin sat and scoured over the pages of the wedding magazine that Karen put in front of her as she earmarked pages of dresses, shoes, hairstyles and more that she thought would be great for the wedding. She already noted several items that she liked while Karen worked on creating a detailed list of who she wanted to invite to their big day.

"Karen, have you guys picked a date yet? We're looking at all this stuff and selecting items, but you need to know what day you are going to try to do all this," Kristin remarked.

"We're going for May 22nd," Karen said casually, writing more things down on her notepad.

"So, you have a little more than 2 months to do all of this? You are nuts. I don't know how you can pull it all together that fast."

"Stop panicking, Kris. We have it under control. We're going to use the hall at the VFW for the reception. I already booked it. Brian knows someone at the restaurant who offered to take care of the catering and everything, so we have the food all set. I'm going to talk to Father Griffin at the church tomorrow to see about having the ceremony there if it's free. If not, we can just get married outside somewhere. It will all work out, I promise. You're more worried about it than I am."

Karen went back to looking at her contacts list on her laptop and wrote names down while Kristin flipped through some more pages of the magazine. The two were silent for a minute or two before Karen looked over her computer screen at Kristin.

"You know, we haven't talked about last night," Karen offered. "How was Wes this morning?"

Kristin flipped through some pages faster now.

"I don't know. He wasn't awake when I left, and he slept down in the entertainment room last night."

Karen nodded and waited for Kristin to tell her more, but Kristin didn't offer anything. Kristin peered at Karen and flashed one of the pages she was looking at to her.

"How about this one?" Kristin asked, showing her the flowing wedding dress.

"Not enough cleavage," Karen said. "So, you guys haven't talked at all?"

Kristin put the magazine down.

"Karen, he was out of line last night. I get he drank too much too fast, but the way he talked to me, and to you and Brian, was unacceptable, and then the way he behaved after you guys left… well, I am still mad about it."

"I get it," Karen answered. "But you know Wes is a great guy, and maybe he just had a bad night. Goodness knows I've had too much to drink and perhaps said or did things I shouldn't have done, and you still talk to me."

"It's not that I won't talk to Wes again, Karen. You know that. But it was all very frustrating for me, and still is. I know he hasn't been happy, but he also hasn't let me in to do anything, to support him, or help him out. And then he lashes out at Izzy or me when he can't handle it."

"Is that why you hadn't told him about my engagement?" Karen asked.

Kristin sat back in her chair and looked at Karen.

"There are a couple of reasons why I didn't," Kristin admitted. "First is that we have hardly had a conversation in weeks. Every time I try to talk to him about anything, he just gives me short answers or says nothing at all. Second… and please don't take this the wrong way… I think I was a little angry that you got engaged."

"Angry?" Karen said with surprise. "At me? Why?"

"Not so much at you, but at the whole thing. You were right when we talked about marriage and all that, and you told me about your engagement. I think part of me was jealous that it was you who got engaged and not me, and maybe I held that against Wes as well."

Karen just looked at Kristin without a response.

"I know," Kristin stated to break the silence. "It's petty and unfair, and it has nothing really to do with you."

"Hey," Karen told Kristin as Karen rose from the table and stood next to her friend. "I was as shocked as anybody that I got engaged. To be honest, I thought you and Wes would have done it long ago. You guys are so in love and so good together, it just seems natural. Have… have you talked to Wes about any of this?"

"No, Kristin said dejectedly. "It's on the growing list of things that we haven't talked about."

"Sounds to me like you two have a lot you need to go over."

Karen leaned down and put her arms around Kristin to hug her.

"All this stuff can wait, Kris. You and I can get together and talk about dresses and stuff any day. You should probably go and talk to Wes and straighten all this out."

"Are you sure?" Kristin asked, but Karen just nodded and smiled.

Kristin rose from her chair and gave Karen a tighter hug.

"Thanks for listening," Kristin told Karen. "I'll talk to you later. Maybe we can get together tomorrow to do this."

"If everything goes well between you and Wes," Karen replied, "and I think it will, you'll be too busy tomorrow. I'll see you at work on Monday."

Kristin laughed, for the first time all day, and walked out of Karen's place and straight to her car. She made the short drive through the heart of Chandler to get to Route 5 and toward the house. Before she could get far up the driveway and drove in front of Wes' parents' house, she saw Wes coming down the hill in his Jeep. The two vehicles stopped, faced each other, and Wes and Kristin spent a moment staring at each other through the windshields of their cars. Kristin recognized the look on Wes' face, and she knew right away he felt terrible about how he acted. She gave him a sly smile and turned her car off before she hopped out.

Wes followed suit and climbed out of his car and paused in front of Kristin in no time at all.

"Can you forgive me for being an ass?" Wes said as he gazed down into Kristin's eyes.

"Of course, I can," Kristin told him. "But Wes, you… I mean we… need to be better about talking to each other about what is going on. I know I should have been more open to you, and told you about things like Karen's engagement and the incident at the meeting with Fred, and for that I am sorry, but you…"

Wes interrupted Kristin and put a finger up to her lips.

"I haven't been the easiest person to live with lately. It's been like a broken record with me getting all moody like this, and I am going to do my best to work through all this, I promise. And I will let you know what I am going through, feeling and thinking."

Wes and Kristin embraced, and the hug quickly turned into a passionate kiss. Kristin leaned against the front of her car as she and Wes kissed deeply again and again before they stopped. Wes rested his forehead against Kristin's.

"Want to know what I am thinking right now?" he said with raised eyebrows.

"What are you thinking, Mr. Martin?" Kristin replied.

"I'm thinking Izzy is out of the house for the rest of the day and we have the whole place to ourselves. Maybe I can fix us some lunch, light a fire in the fireplace, put on some romantic music…"

Wes began to lightly kiss Kristin on the neck, working his way down to the nape where his bit of stubble tickled Kristin and caused her to giggle.

The romantic mood and quiet were quickly broken by a voice from nearby.

"Do you two mind not making out and blocking my driveway?" Wyatt remarked from the front porch. "I need to drive down to the stables to work."

Kristin peered over Wes' shoulder, smiling at Wyatt before Wes stood up and looked at his father.

"Sure, Dad, thanks," Wes said, giving a wave. He gave Kristin another peck on the lips before he raced back towards his car. Wes drove up the hill in reverse rapidly, and the vehicle kicked up mud and melted snow along the way.

"Glad to see you two talking," Wyatt told Kristin as he got into his pickup truck.

"Thank you, Wyatt," Kristin replied before she jumped into her own vehicle to catch up to Wes and get into the house as fast as she could. All the while, she thought that everything began to fall back into place.

10

All remnants of the snow melted away swiftly as temperatures warmed for early March. Wes heard the birds chirping happily as he walked up to the batting cage complex in the mornings. His legs and arms strengthened with each passing day, and Wes' vision and the way he tracked the ball pitched was as keen as it had been during his playing days. He spent more time not only working on his hitting but working out in his home gym to get in even better shape. Muscle tone returned to his body, and the firmness of his abs appeared as prominent as before.

With all the positives coming from the workouts and practice, this should have been a much better time for Wes. Unfortunately, even with all the drills and good signs in his hitting, Wes still felt incomplete. He hadn't heard from his agent Randy since that initial phone call where Wes indicated his interest in coming back. Wes didn't want to pester Randy every day, but he expected to at least to be kept abreast of what was going on.

After his morning workout, Wes plodded back down to the house to shower. Once he washed the day's workout away, he wrapped a towel around his waist and strode into the bedroom. Wes reached for his cellphone and instinctively checked for any messages or emails. Disappointment reigned when he saw nothing again. Instead of tossing the phone onto the bed or smashing it against the wall like he felt like doing, Wes scrolled through his contacts, found Randy, and pressed call.

Randy's assistant Tammy kept Wes on hold for a bit, which made Wes wonder if Randy attempted to try to dodge his call. Randy did things like this in the past, even when Wes sat in the room with him, so it wouldn't be a big surprise to find himself on the other end of that treatment, but Wes hoped that his years of loyalty to Randy, and all the money he helped Randy make, still counted for something.

"Hey Wes, what's going on?" Randy chimed in, taking Wes by surprise.

"Hey, Randy. I... I just wanted to check in with you and see if you had heard anything," Wes answered with some hesitation.

Randy remained quiet for a moment, something he didn't often do, and Wes knew it meant he searched for the right words of what to say.

"It hasn't been that long, Wes. You need to give it some more time."

"Randy, the season starts in just over two weeks. I'm running out of time. I've felt great, the hitting is there, and I'm in fantastic shape. I've even taken fielding practice with the local high school team when I get the chance and have shagged some flies in the outfield. Now, I know I haven't played outfield in a long time, but I think..."

Randy interrupted Wes abruptly.

"Wes, look, I'm sorry. I've made the rounds, talked to GMs, owners, and anyone that might listen. There's... there's just nothing out there right now."

Wes had trouble comprehending the notion.

"Come on, Randy. I know some teams out there that are having trouble at first base or need a DH or even just a guy off the bench. The Pirates still don't really have anybody for one."

"Wes, Pittsburgh was my first call," Randy explained. "I figured if anyone would have interest it was them, but they said they want to get younger right now."

"Okay, that's fine," Wes retorted. "There are 29 other teams out there to look at. Chicago, Texas, LA… hell, Miami is always looking for older guys to fill out their bench."

"There's no right way for me to say this Wes, so I'm just going to say it. Your name has been out there, and… and there just aren't any takers. Teams are rounding out the rosters now, and no one seems ready to take a flyer on you."

"I don't get it," Wes said with frustration and confusion. "I have good stats, Randy, better than a lot of the guys you see on teams today. You're telling me no one is willing to bite at all? If it's a money thing, I will take the minimum. I don't care about the salary; I just want to play."

"It's not the salary, Wes," Randy tried to be as gentle as possible with what he had to say. "You're thirty-six, and you only played two games last year. To be honest, teams worry about how you walked away last year. They don't want to take the risk of you taking a roster spot, playing for a few weeks or even a month or two, and then you change your mind again and leave."

"Come on, no one really said that to you," Wes answered.

"More than one GM told me that, Wes," Randy stated.

"What happened to everyone thinking it was such a wonderful thing that I chose my family over a big salary?" Wes' tone sparked with annoyance.

"The press is the one that eats that stuff up, Wes. You know that. The teams only care about wins and profit. Cincinnati and Pittsburgh may have said all the right things when you retired last year like that, but the bottom line is that it doesn't mean anything to them now. You left, they celebrated you a bit, but now they have moved on, and so have the other teams, the press, and the fans. You coming back now makes people wonder what's going on, if you need the money, if there are problems at home... there aren't problems at home, are there? You know you can tell me the truth, Wes."

"Randy, there aren't any problems at home." It was a bit of a white lie, but Randy didn't need to know about the issues he faced with Kristin right now. "I just want to play baseball again."

The two men remained silent on the phone for ten seconds, though to Wes it seemed like two hours.

"What... what about a minor league deal?" Wes added.

"Wes, you really want to do that?" Randy couldn't believe Wes even mentioned the minors.

"The minors mean a low salary, but it also means everything that goes along with it – travel by bus, cheap hotels, lousy meals, no frills, and there are no guarantees that it will even lead to something. And suppose it doesn't work out and you don't play well? You want the press all over you getting released by some AAA team so they can write about what a mistake it all was? I think it's a bad idea."

Wes was quiet again as he considered what Randy said. It was all true, and Wes knew it, but his desires right now were stronger than ever, and the willingness to swallow his pride if it came down to that surged.

"Randy, I know if I get a chance, I can prove them all wrong. Please… I just need a shot."

The apparent desperation in Wes' voice shone through to Randy.

"Okay, Wes," Randy said resignedly. "Let me see what I can find out. I can call a few more people and see if anything is out there, but I can't make you any promises, Wes. You have to be aware of that and willing to accept it."

"I know," Wes conceded. "Thanks, Randy, I appreciate it. Just, keep me posted, okay?"

"Will do, buddy," Randy told him before he hung up.

Wes tossed the phone on the bed and lay back. He stretched himself out as he let out a big sigh. He never expected it to be this hard, trying to come back. After hitting nothing but home runs in his at-bats last season and captivating the baseball world, he thought for sure there would be at least one team willing to give him a tryout and maybe a bench job. The process was a much more significant blow to his ego than he anticipated.

It didn't help that Randy mentioned the notion about there being trouble at home. Wes wasn't at his best, he acknowledged that and there had been rough patches with Kristin and with Izzy, but he thought he had smoothed all that out. His mood improved since he had been practicing more and the relationships with everyone were better than they had been in months, weren't they?

Wes stared up at the motionless ceiling fan above the bed, and suddenly there was a kinship between Wes and this device he rarely noticed or considered. They were both stuck, waiting for the spring, for the chance to show how useful they both could be to all around them.

****

Kristin opened the windows in her office to allow the breeze to flow through and get some of the stale air out that built up over the long winter. Having the light wind come across her face now and then was enough to make her sit back in her chair, close her eyes, and smile. A freshness came in and made everything much better.

Work had been tense for a bit after the last board meeting, and Marion remained in constant contact with her since the incident with Fred Clark. Marion repeatedly told Kristin that the board took her feelings seriously and worked towards what steps to take, which gave Kristin little satisfaction. To make things worse, word had spread fast around Chandler about what was said at the board meeting. Small town gossip always blew things out of proportion, and more than one person mentioned it to Kristin. While most of the younger women that approached Kristin about the incident took her side, the older women in town, and indeed the older men, all seemed to feel that she overreacted and appeared too thin-skinned about it and should just let it go.

Kristin wanted nothing more to let it go and put it behind her so she could get through a day without it coming up, but she also wanted to make sure that Fred and others in town knew what he said was insensitive, out of touch, sexist and wrong. Kristin closed more than one conversation, post, and comments on the library's Facebook page because people kept bringing it up and it ended with arguments, unrest, and a lot of childish behavior and name-calling. She never expected things to get to this point.

While Kristin was going over her latest request list to see what new releases she would bring into the library, her desk phone rang. It was her private line, not the general phone line for the library, an unusual occurrence. Wes, Izzy, or Wes' parents or her own family always called her cell phone if they needed her. Kristin sat up and cleared her throat before answering.

"Kristin Arthur," she stated in her friendliest yet professional tone.

"Kristin, it is Marion Harris," Marion said, taking her own professional demeanor in response. Kristin's hand tensed around the phone, and she tried to do relaxation breathing to calm herself. Lately, any time she spoke with Marion, anxiety ruled the moment.

"Hi, Marion. What can I do for you?" Kristin's teeth clenched.

"I was wondering if we could get together and speak for a little bit?"

"Of course," Kristin answered. "Why don't you come down to my office?"

"I would prefer to do this outside of the library if we could. Do you think you could come over to my home so we could meet in my office? We'll have more privacy there."

"Your... your house?" Kristin said nervously. She had never been asked to Marion's home before.

"Yes," Marion answered. "Can you get here in about 15 minutes? I know it's last minute, but I do have other appointments today, and this needs to be taken care of as soon as possible. Do you need the address?"

"No, I mean 15 minutes is fine, and I know where the house is," Kristin replied.

"Excellent. I'll see you shortly." Marion promptly hung up, and Kristin held her phone for a moment in stunned silence.

Kristin put down the receiver and reclined in her chair. Worry coursed through her as she wondered what Marion wanted that couldn't be said over the phone or in the library. It clearly meant a sensitive topic, which made it all appear worse to Kristin. Kristin quickly gathered her purse and jacket and went out into the library.

Karen sat perched at her stool at the front desk while she scanned some recent returns into the system. Karen turned her head when she saw Kristin standing there.

"Where are you going?" Karen inquired. "It's a little early to knock off for the day, but more power to you, Boss," Karen said with a smirk.

Kristin walked closer to Karen so she could whisper without those in the library hearing the conversation.

"No, Marion just called me. She asked me to come out to her house for a talk."

Karen slammed a stack of books down onto the counter, which caused heads to lift like meerkats to see what was going on.

"Her house? What the hell for? She better not be thinking of firing you over this whole thing. If she does, I'm walking too," Karen said forcefully.

"I don't know what she wants," Kristin began. Kristin straightened up and looked at Karen. "If she does want to fire me, well that's her choice, but I'm not going down without having my say. I'll be sure to give her a piece of my mind. And you shouldn't quit even if she does fire me, Karen. You need the job. Think about yourself and don't worry about me."

Karen reached over and grabbed Kristin's hand.

"Give 'em hell!" Karen thundered, evoking the meerkat response again.

Kristin strode out of the library, holding her head up and not looking at any of the patrons as she left. She marched right to her car in the small parking lot, got behind the wheel and made the right turn to head down Main Street.

Everyone in town knew which house was Marion Harris'. The large Victorian home was positioned at the far end of Main Street, the last building there before Main Street turned to Route 15 and headed out into the more rural areas of Chandler. Kristin could have easily walked to Marion's home, but she knew that pacing the few blocks over would make her more anxious about the meeting. She wanted to get there and get this over with as quickly as possible.

In just over a half a mile, Kristin turned through the open wrought-iron gate to go up the short circular driveway to the home. Marion's family continued as something of a legacy in Chandler, even more so than the Martins. Marion's maiden name was Chandler, and she was a direct descendant of the founders of the town. She married Victor Harris back in the late 1950s, and Victor, a noted banker, and financier in the area, had passed away some twenty years ago, leaving Marion even wealthier than her family name left her. She moved back to the Chandler house, restored it to its former glory, and spent all her time engaged in social activities and philanthropic endeavors.

Kristin parked her vehicle at the top of the circle driveway outside the house. It was the only car visible since the house vehicles resided safely in a nearby garage. Kristin climbed the stone steps to the porch and rang the bell, listening to the chimes echo inside.

An older woman answered, clearly Marion's housekeeper, and smiled at Kristin.

"I'm… I'm Kristin Arthur. I'm here to see Mrs. Harris," Kristin said, fumbling with her words.

"Of course," the woman replied politely and waved Kristin inside.

The entryway immediately reminded Kristin of <u>Gone with the Wind</u> with its sweeping staircase and décor. A large chandelier hung overhead that made the room brighter than it needed to be, and all Kristin could think of when she looked at it was that it must be a pain in the ass to clean or change a light bulb for whatever staff that chore fell to.

The housekeeper fluttered with Kristin through room after room, so much so that Kristin thought she might have a hard time if she needed to find her way back out of the house once the meeting with Marion ended. They finally reached Marion's office, a spacious spot that might put the Oval Office to shame. Kristin couldn't believe the floor-to-ceiling bookcases, the antique desk at the center of the room, the wondrous tapestries, and the gold birdcage with a colorful macaw eating seeds.

Kristin took a seat in the plush chair opposite the large desk and suddenly felt like the naughty schoolgirl that had been called to the principal's office.

"Mrs. Harris will be in shortly. Can I get you something to drink?" the housekeeper politely stated.

"Oh, no, thank you," Kristin responded.

The housekeeper gave Kristin a gentle half-bow and made her way from the room. Kristin couldn't help herself and needed to go look at the rows of books that adorned the bookcases. There was a ladder much like they had at the library so that you could get to the books on the upper shelves. Kristin always dreamed of having a room in her house like this, where she could escape to and relax, curled up in a cozy chair by the fireplace so that she could get lost in whatever she chose to read that day.

Kristin let her hand gently glide over the spines of the books in front of her. Many of the books looked antiquated, and she guessed some were easily a hundred years old or more. She was tempted to just take one off the shelf to look at it but was afraid she might damage it or set off some silent alarm that would have guards rush in with guns drawn at her.

"Ahhh, I knew you would appreciate my office," the proper voice beckoned from behind her. Kristin gave a startled shake, and her hand jumped back from the books as she spun around to see Marion.

Marion entered the room further, and Kristin watched as the housekeeper pulled the doors closed.

"Your library is amazing," Kristin commented as she paced back over to the chair. Marion took a seat behind her desk and smiled.

"Thank you, dear. My family has always had a great love of books. One of my ancestors started the town library. Many of those you see here are first editions, some from my grandfather and great-grandfather. I need to keep supporting reading, which is why I take my role at the library so seriously."

Marion's face turned serious and stern. Kristin worried about what might come next, but she prepared to defend herself vigorously if needed.

"Marion, I just want to say before you state anything that I feel I have done an excellent job taking care of the library and helping it grow. My passions are books and reading, and I do all I can to foster that within our community. As for what happened at the board meeting, I held my tongue and did not lash out at Fred Clark as I could have and should have for his remarks, and I don't feel I should be punished for what he said or did. If that's the way you want to go and run things, then perhaps I am not the best fit for the library after all."

Kristin trembled and sat on her hands to keep the visible shaking hidden from Marion. Kristin surprised herself that she got out her statement without passing out on the floor. She looked up at Marion and saw that the older woman just stared back at her. After about ten seconds that felt more like an hour to Kristin, Marion leaned back in her chair and smiled.

"Did you think I asked you here so that I could tell you we were letting you go? Don't be ridiculous, dear. I think you have done a fantastic job with our library, and you have been a great asset for us. I did ask you to come here so we could talk about that meeting, though. I wanted to apologize again for Fred's behavior. I am sure you understand many people in this town are, shall we say, a bit behind in the times when it comes to their views on women. I understand how difficult it can be for a woman to work hard and earn respect for what she has accomplished. No, dear, I support you wholeheartedly. I just wish some of the others around here would get their heads out of their asses, so to speak."

Kristin exhaled and allowed herself to relax a bit.

"Thank you, Marion. That means a lot to me."

"Now," Marion added, opening a folder on her desk. "The rest of the board and I met this morning, and we voted to ask Fred to step down from his position. After some cajoling on our part, he saw things our way and resigned."

Kristin did not expect that reaction at all. Her past experiences with the board led her to believe they stuck by each other. Moving Fred Clark out was undoubtedly a shocking maneuver.

"Okay," Kristin remarked and nodded, unsure of what else to say.

"Naturally, that left us one position short on the board, and we needed a seventh member to help avoid constant ties in votes. Luckily, we found someone more than willing to step in and help us out. Do you know Dr. Trainor?"

Kristin had heard the name before, but she saw lots of names come across her desk in the course of the day.

"I think I have heard the name before, but I have never met Dr. Trainor."

"Oh, well he has only been in town for a few months," Marion answered. She began to flip through a few of the pages she had in her folder before she set upon Dr. Trainor's information.

"Yes, Dr. Richard Trainor. He's a chiropractor who just opened an office in town back in December. Quite a nice gentleman, just thirty years old, came from a family in Pittsburgh and worked there for a bit before relocating here. He has done some volunteer work with a few of the charities I am associated with, and I believe he will be a good fit for us. He brings in some younger blood to the board."

Kristin smiled, happy to hear the news. Someone younger on the board! That could definitely work to her benefit. Another person that might support newer technology and methods that could broaden the services and appeal of the library would be ideal. She had the chance to implement some new ideas and get the proper funding to make it all happen.

"That sounds good to me," Kristin offered as she worked to hide her excitement. "I would love to get the chance to meet Dr. Trainor. I can give him a call and see if he wants to swing by the library to go over what we do if you would like."

"Oh no need, dear," Marion added, closing her folder. "I already spoke to him and let him know he could just drop by when it is convenient for him. I hope that is okay."

"Certainly," Kristin replied. She had already started going over in her head what she might need to do to get everything organized and ready. It would take some hustling, but Kristin had the confidence that she would make it happen.

"Is there anything else?" Kristin stated anxiously. She wanted to get going to return to the library and start work.

"No, I think that was it," Marion told her. Marion stood up behind her desk and smiled.

"Hopefully we can put some of these things behind us now and get back to doing good work at the library."

"I agree," Kristin said hastily. She stood up and turned to see the housekeeper standing in the doorway as if she had appeared by magic.

"Sonya can show you out," Marion said.

"Thank you, Marion," Kristin said with earnest.

"No, thank you, Kristin, for all the hard work you do. I know you will keep bringing good things to our town. Have a good day, dear."

Marion sat back down at her desk, picking up her reading glasses and placing them on so she could go over some files.

Kristin followed Sonya through the maze of rooms and back to the front door. She reached her car and gave it a light tap on the roof before opening the door to get in. Once inside the car, she let out an exhilarated yell.

"Yes!!" she shouted, loud enough so that the man pruning a tree about twenty yards away turned and looked at her to make sure everything was alright. Kristin blushed and started her car, heading back to the library parking lot and feeling good about the way things were going for the first time in weeks.

11

When Wes took his steps out onto the back lawn for his daily trek to the batting cage, the ground was much firmer, having dried out from days of warmth and sunshine. The sun warmed his skin, and he quickly found no need for the sweatshirt he put on before he left the house. The constant string of warm days meant that spring indeed appeared, but it also said that the start of baseball season loomed precariously close.

Wes pushed open the door to the batting cage and went inside, turned the lights on and got everything started. While the cage felt cooler inside than the temperature outside, he had no need to even put heat on to warm things up today. That thought alone had him going right into the batting area to start to hit.

Wes took thunderous, angry swings each time the ball came in. He couldn't hit the ball hard enough for his liking. It had been over a week since he last talked to Randy about a team that would give him a tryout or even a minor league spot to start out with. More than once he had been tempted to pick up the phone and call Randy, only to put it back down, almost fearful of what the answer would be from Randy to his question about what was going on.

Line drive after line drive leaped off his bat, and the pitches Wes did miss he practically screwed himself into the ground he swung so hard. He chased curveballs that were slower and out of the zone, and he wanted to crush anything that came his way. He knew it was the wrong approach, and as frustrating as it was to miss pitch after pitch, he didn't care. Wes swung at every ball that came in and tried to drive the ball through the netting at the back of the batting cage no matter what.

The timer went off and buzzed in the air to signal the end of the session Wes created. He didn't need to look at the computer to let know he failed to have a good session. Wes flung his bat to the ground, grabbed his towel and phone, and flipped the power off. He slammed the door shut behind him as he left. He marched down the hill and went into the house, heading right to the bathroom to shower.

Wes climbed in and just let the water run over his body continuously. He hung his head right under the showerhead and closed his eyes so tightly that just dark colors and flashes coursed through his eyelids.

This wasn't how it was supposed to be, he told himself.

After just standing under the water for minutes on end, Wes opened his eyes and washed off. The shower and the bathroom filled with heavy steam by the time he finished. Wes grabbed a towel and dried off, then tossed the towel angrily to the floor before going back to the bedroom naked. He sat back on the bed and glanced over at the nightstand to see that the screen on his cellphone was lit. Text messages from Kristin dotted the screen.

In the past, the two of them sent messages back and forth often to keep in touch during the day. Lately, that routine died off, particularly with the moods Wes flashed over and over. It had all been on Wes, and he knew it, but lately, there didn't seem to be much of a way to get out of it. The messages from Kristin usually stated things like she was going to be late or had to pick up Izzy that day and what would they do for dinner instead of the fun, flirty or romantic notes of the past.

Today's message didn't read much differently. Kristin asked where he was and what he was up to. Wes prepared to respond, but then noticed a couple of phone messages as well. He pressed the button on his phone, and the first message played. It was from Kristin:

"Wes, where are you? I sent you some text messages, and you didn't answer. I just got a call from Randy, and he said he's trying to get in touch with you…"

Wes didn't listen to the rest. He skipped to the end so the next message would play, hoping it was from Randy.

"Wes, it's Randy. Call me back when you get a minute, okay. Thanks."

Randy's voice didn't sound like it had any excitement to it or anything, so Wes couldn't get a good read on what was going on. He hesitated for a moment, but then pressed Call Back to get to Randy.

"Hey, Wes," Randy said after just one ring. "You're a tough man to get a hold of today."

"I was just up hitting. Nothing exciting," Wes answered. "What's going on?"

Wes tried not to show any hint of anticipation in his voice. He wanted to be prepared for whatever it is Randy told him, good or bad.

"I'm sorry I haven't gotten back to you sooner," Randy began. "I've made calls for you left and right, and talked to all kinds of people and connections."

There was a bit of silence on the phone after that.

"And?" Wes asked.

"I haven't been able to get anyone to bite just yet, majors or minors. There's… there's nothing there."

"If you've been trying to chase me down just to tell me that Randy, I can't say I'm pleased about it. There's nothing urgent about that."

Dejection overwhelmed Wes at this point as he paced the room.

"Well, I do have one thing…" Randy added as his voice tapered off a bit.

"What is it?" Wes said excitedly.

"Wes, keep in mind…"

"Randy, get to it!" Wes interrupted.

"Okay, are you familiar with the Washington Wild Things?"

The name raced through Wes' mind as he thought about minor league teams.

"The name doesn't ring a bell. Who are they affiliated with? The Nationals?"

"No, different Washington," Randy responded.

"Seattle?" Wes cut in again.

"No, not there either. Look, Wes, the Washington Wild Things are an independent baseball team in the Frontier League. They play in Washington, Pennsylvania, not far from you. I know it's not what you wished for, but I gave them a call. When I told them you were looking to play this year, they got very excited about having you. A local guy, big-league experience, it would be great for their team."

"Independent ball?" Wes said softly.

Independent ball. The last bastion of the truly desperate professional. Most of the players were guys who played college ball that weren't good enough for the minors and wanted a shot somewhere; at least that's how Wes thought about it.

"Hey, it's not luxurious, that's for sure. Truthfully Wes, if you want to play ball, this is probably your only shot," Randy said solemnly.

"What about… what about if I wait it out, stay in shape," Wes responded. "It could be like last year. Someone might get hurt, they might want a solid replacement."

"Sure, we could do that, Wes. The difference is last year you had been at spring training the whole time and missed only a week. You haven't played in a year now. Teams don't know what they will get from you and will be reluctant to take a chance. At least if you play independent ball, you are playing. If someone is interested, then they have somewhere to go and watch you play to see what you have got."

Wes stroked his cheeks, feeling the stubble as he pondered what to do.

"Do I have to decide right now?" Wes asked.

"No, you don't," Randy answered. "They don't start playing until later in the spring, so you have some time. I'm pretty sure they would take you no matter what. They are just excited about the opportunity. Talk it over with the family and get back to me when you are ready."

"Thanks, Randy." Wes tried to hide the disappointment in his voice.

"No problem, buddy. Let me know if you need anything, or just want to talk, okay?"

"Yeah, will do. Thanks again." Wes hung up and realized he had wandered out into the kitchen while he was talking to Randy. He placed the phone down on the counter, opened the fridge, and grabbed the bottle of orange juice he saw in there. Without a thought, he twisted the top off and took a drink from the container.

Wes' phone buzzed, indicating another text message. It was from Kristin.

Did you talk to Randy? What did he say?

****

The library buzzed with people as the crowd gathered. Kristin lined up a few local authors to come in and read and then have a Q & A with the audience, advertising it as a 'meet the local authors' day. She set up readings to go on all day, with different genres throughout to draw in people most interested in a particular type of book. The early parts of the day included a few children's authors to bring in Moms and Dads with young kids, and the turnout exceeded what Kristin could have hoped for. She made sure to have some beverages and snacks on hand, donated by the local bakery, and she and Karen moved more chairs over to the kids' section where they had everything set up for the event to accommodate everyone.

In between the constant run around, the coordination of the events for the day, talking to authors, visitors to the library, and more, she found herself fielding text messages from Randy, Wes' agent. Kristin met Randy several times, but they were hardly what she would consider close. It startled her to hear from him at first, and when she didn't respond immediately to his messages, her phone began to buzz. She always answered right away, in case it was Wes' parents or Izzy, and this time she didn't even look to see who it was before answering.

"Kristin, hi, it's Randy… Wes' agent."

"Hi, Randy," Kristin said hurriedly. "It's nice to hear from you, but I'm kind of busy right now. Can I call you back in about an hour or so? Or maybe you can try Wes' line?"

"Well, that's kind of what I'm calling about," Randy told her. "I've tried to get in touch with Wes for a while, and he hasn't answered. Do you know where he might be?"

"Honestly, Randy, I don't if he's not answering. He could be at his parents, up at the batting cage, in the shower. Maybe he just doesn't want to talk. He's done a lot of that lately."

Kristin realized what slipped out of her mouth and wished she could take it back right away.

"Is everything okay?" Randy asked concernedly. "I know he's going through a rough patch right now, but I didn't realize it was affecting you two as well."

"It's… well, it's complicated, Randy, and I really don't have the privacy or the time to get into it right now."

Kristin placed down a stack of children's books at one of the author tables and then made her way to her office to grab some pens and Sharpies so the authors could sign items people wanted. She held up two fingers to Karen, who walked by, escorting one of the writers so they could begin, mouthing "2 minutes" to Karen as she slid by.

Kristin reached her office and closed the door, sitting down in her desk chair to take a quick sip of her tepid coffee.

"I'm sorry to bother you while you're working, I really am, I was just... well, I'm worried about Wes," Randy had hesitated before he let Kristin know his concerns.

"You and me both," Kristin answered honestly. "Randy, I wish I knew what I could do to make him feel better. This all came out of the blue. He never gave me any hint that he was unhappy or wanted to play again. Now the closer the season gets the more withdrawn and unhappy it seems. I hope you're looking for him to tell him some good news."

"Well, not completely," Randy told her. "I know how badly he wants to play right now. I've seen this with other clients I have. Retiring when you are still in your thirties, it can be tough to deal with. Once you are out of playing for a little bit, your body and mind miss all that you had, and you feel like maybe you can still do it. It's not easy to just put that aside and pick up with another life."

"I get it, Randy, but I thought he had started the next chapter, with his parents, and Izzy... and with me. I don't know what to do or how to do it at this point."

A knock on Kristin's office door interrupted the brief quiet on the phone. Karen peeked her head in.

"Kris," she whispered, "we're ready to start."

"Okay, I'm coming," Kristin responded.

"Randy, I really have to go. Try his cell again. I'm guessing he's around and just hasn't seen that you are reaching out to him yet. Let me know if you still can't reach him, or if you think there is anything I should know or do that can help."

"Okay, thanks, Kristin. Bye." Randy hung up, leaving Kristin sitting in her chair.

She typed out a quick message to Wes again, to tell him that Randy tried to reach him before she headed out to listen to Karen introduce the author to the crowd, who responded with nice applause.

Kristin stood towards the back of the crowd, to take everything in. She watched as the author read her book, which was an A to Z book all about China, with a dragon that took a little boy on a journey through the country to introduce him to different things. The author did different voices and brought the book to life, and the kids and parents enjoyed it immensely. Kristin smiled and laughed along with the crowd, happy it went so well.

"The crowd really seems to enjoy it," a voice said from next to her.

Kristin gave a bit of a start and didn't realize someone stood next to her. She turned quickly to see the gentleman there, as he watched the author and her. He stood straight and smiled at her, or more down at her since he was much taller. His smile got more full, and he nodded at Kristin, then turned back towards the author.

"Yes, they do," Kristin said politely. "She's very engaging, and it's a fun book, so it's a great combination."

"You've done a great job with this event, Ms. Arthur," the man said to her.

Kristin shot him a look, getting a side glance of the impeccably groomed dark beard he had to match his well-manicured haircut.

"I'm sorry, do we know each other?"

"Well, not formally," he said. He rotated back towards Kristin and offered his hand. "I'm Richard Trainor, the new member of the library board."

"Oh, Dr... Trainor, yes, Marion mentioned you to me. It's nice to meet you."

Kristin placed her hand in his to shake it. He had firm, strong hands, and Kristin took a quick look to see that his nails were better-taken care of than her own. He shook her hand and then glided it away. His fingers lingered over the tips of her fingers before she could pull her hand away.

"Please, call me Richard. I get enough of the mister and doctor stuff all day long. I'm sorry I didn't come by sooner or call you to let you know I was coming by, but I thought this would be a good day to see you in action, as it were. I've seen flyers all over town and on the town Facebook page announcing the event. You've done a great job getting the community to support you."

"Thank you, I appreciate that... Richard," Kristin said. She noticed his dark brown eyes and the piercing look that they gave. "I think the library is one of the town's great assets and we have so much more to offer."

"I agree," he told her as he attempted to keep his voice down as the reading continued. "I'd like the opportunity to talk to you some more about what your plans are and what you would like to do. Marion mentioned you had a lot of ideas."

Kristin's eyes lit up. She had the chance to get the ear of a board member now and maybe have someone that could sway the other members to let her try some new things here.

"That would be great," Kristin said excitedly.

The crowd broke out in applause as the author finished reading, capturing Kristin's attention again.

"I have to go up there," she said, pointing to the author's table. "Why don't you give me a call here at the library and we can set something up. Things are a bit hectic over the next few days, but I think maybe we can fit something in."

"I'll have to check my appointment schedule," Richard replied. "I'm pretty busy most days at my practice. Lots of people needing help and adjustments in this town. Do you think you could give me your cell number? It might be easier for me to reach you off-hours or send you a text."

"Sure, that would be fine." Kristin reached into the pocket of the cardigan she wore and pulled out a yellow Post-It pad and pen. She scribbled down her number and handed it to Richard, who took the note quickly and looked at it, smiling.

"Great, it was nice to meet you. I look forward to seeing you again and working with you."

Richard nodded at her as Kristin moved off towards the author, who sat at the table now as she got ready to sign books. Kristin glanced over her shoulder and noticed Richard still watching her as she walked. She arrived at the table and Karen greeted her there, handing a stack of books over to her to put in front of the author.

"Who's that?" Karen asked, watching Richard as he turned and headed for the door.

"Richard Trainor," Kristin told her. "He's the new board member. He has a chiropractic practice down the road. He came in to introduce himself."

"Seems a little... intense," Karen said. "What do you mean? He seemed fine to me." Kristin finished arranging things on the table before Karen pulled her off to the side so the author could begin signing.

"I guess," Karen shrugged. "I saw the two of you talking. He never took his eyes off you. Then, when you walked up here, he kept following you. It just felt weird to me."

"I think you're reading too much into it, Karen," Kristin said, not thinking much about it. "He might be the chance we have to get some more programs and funding for the library. Young blood on that board is what we need most right now if we want any hope of change around here."

"Okay, you're the boss," Karen said with a salute.

Kristin smiled at the gesture.

"We've got about 20 minutes before the next author. I'm going to go set up things over by the computers. The next one is a guy who wrote a cybersecurity book."

Kristin walked over to the computer area where a couple of people had already come in to take seats. She arranged a few of the extra folding chairs she had around the area and wheeled over the small podium they had for the speaker. She took a moment and rested her hands on the podium. Pride coursed through her once more, before her thoughts returned to Wes and what he faced. She pulled her cell phone out of her cardigan pocket and zipped off another message to Wes to ask if he had spoken with Randy yet.

I hope he's having as good of a day as I am, Kristin thought.

12

Wes spent the better part of the rest of the day in thought about what his decision would be. There were upsides to the opportunity. The team location made it so he wouldn't be far from home, and it would allow him to get seen by scouts and other clubs that might be willing to pick him up. He was sure he could do enough to impress someone that his stay in independent ball wouldn't be too long if he took it. Even the salary didn't matter since he had done well as a major-league player and saved a lot of money over the years.

Wes had done a little research on the Frontier League since his discussion with Randy. The teams all played in the same part of the country, though the Wild Things were the team furthest east. Wes knew this meant travel west for hours, and travel by bus, something he hadn't done since his days in the minors nearly twenty years ago. Most of the players would be significantly younger than him, with the average age closer to Kristin's than his by a long shot. And there was another age problem as well. Frontier League rules recently changed so that no one over the age of 27 could play on a team. Wes became crestfallen reading that. There went his shot, but why would the club say they had interest in him if they knew about the rule?

After doing his research, Wes picked up the phone and called Randy again. He needed more answers. Wes was surprised when Randy picked up his own office phone.

"Why are you answering your phone?" Wes asked.

"Oh, Tammy was out running a few errands. That girl is something else. The best hire I have made in a long time. Anyway… so what's going on? Do you have a decision for me? The sooner I can get back to the team, the better, you know."

"Well, I have a few questions first," Wes said as he paced around the bedroom. "The biggest thing is the age thing. Did you know they have an age rule? No one over 27. That should nix everything before we even start."

"I did know about it," Randy said. "The team said they were going to talk to the league office to see if they could get a waiver of the rule for you. They seemed pretty sure the league would go for it. They haven't had a star player to hang their hat on, and the whole league might get a boost in attendance everywhere you go with you there. I think it's just a formality, but you have to give the okay before they decide to move forward with it."

"Am I going to be more than just a sideshow attraction for them, Randy? They know I want to play, right?"

"They know, Wes, but you have to see it from their point of view too. They want the attention it brings. You both get something out of the deal. Hey, you knew it was going to be this way if you went to anything other than the majors right away. That's the reality of it, Wes. If you really want to play badly enough, you're going to have to put up with it. I'm sorry, but that's the way it is. You don't have to say yes to it."

Randy had laid it all for Wes as plainly as possible.

"Any other questions?" Randy said, breaking the quiet.

"Nope, I think that's it," Wes stated. Wes walked downstairs and sat on the couch. He looked up and stared at the blank big screen TV.

"So, what do you think?" Randy pressed for some type of answer.

"Tell them yes," Wes announced.

"Really? You don't want more time to think about it? Maybe talk things over with Kristin and Izzy more?"

"No, I think we're good. Just let me know what the next steps are. Thanks, Randy." Wes hung up before Randy had the chance to say anything that might get him to change his mind.

Wes blurted out his decision without a second thought. It was what he wanted to do, but a hint of guilt crept into his body. He didn't talk about the decision with Kristin, Izzy, his parents, or with anyone. Would they see it as a selfish move? He felt strongly that they would tell him they supported him, but would they say that just to appease him? Wes had been enough of a jerk lately that even he realized he acted that way, and this might push things over the edge.

Wes considered calling Randy back to pull out of the entire thing. He could stay retired, enjoy life, work on the farm, do charitable events like the library, maybe show up for some Old-Timer's Day games, do memorabilia shows, or anything else that might keep him connected to the game. That was enough for a lot of other retired players, so why couldn't it be the same for him?

The answer to that question approached the front of Wes' brain instantly. He knew he couldn't be pleased if that's how things played out. He needed certainty, and this was the only way he was going to get it.

"But now I have to convince everyone else of that," Wes said out loud to himself.

****

The last of the crowd left the library, and Karen went and locked the front door. Kristin busied herself and picked up empty coffee cups and paper plates to toss in the trash. The last speaker read from his latest thriller novel and kept the audience on edge, and he was clearly the hit of the event. Kristin made sure to take plenty of pictures with her phone all day long that she could post to social media tomorrow and for the coming days so that people could see what a success the day had been.

"Man, that was some day!" Karen exclaimed. "We must have had everyone in town come through here at some point. Look at all the names we got signed up for our mailing lists, too. You knocked this one out of the park, Kris."

The baseball analogy wasn't lost on Kristin.

"Yeah, well, *we* kicked ass today," Kristin said with a smirk. "Thanks for all your hard work, Karen. You went above and beyond today."

"Hey, I was happy to do it. We're a team you know. Of course, it's going to take us half the night to get this place put back together," Karen said as she surveyed the library.

Kristin placed the last of the garbage she saw in the bag and pulled it out of the trash can.

"Let's leave the rest for tomorrow. It's just putting chairs back and breaking down tables. All the garbage is done. We can clean up and vacuum in the morning. I'm ready to call it a night," Kristin announced.

"Are you sure?" Karen asked.

Kristin held up her wrist and looked at her watch.

"It's already after 9, Karen. Just go home. I'm going to turn off my computer and gather up my stuff, and then I am out of here. I'll close up."

"You're not going to stay and do all this by yourself, are you, Kris?" Karen asked, raising an eyebrow.

"No way," Kristin told her. "I need your muscles to do the tables with me."

Karen gave a quick flex of her biceps to show off.

"Okay, that sounds good. Now I'll get home in time to get Brian to drive down and see me tonight. He's probably just getting off work. I'll see you in the morning, Kris. Great job, boss! Love you!" Karen blew Kristin a kiss and headed for the door as Kristin let out a laugh.

Kristin walked into her office, sat down, and sighed as she kicked off her high heels and rubbed her aching feet through her stockings. She turned her head back and forth to try to work out some of the kinks she felt after a long day on her feet. Kristin grabbed her sneakers out of her bag and slid into them. All she thought about was getting home, getting out of her bra and pantyhose, and kicking back on the bed to relax.

Kristin didn't even take the time to look at her email before she shut her computer down. She picked up her bag and turned off her office lights before making her way to the front door of the library. A few punches on the keypad set the alarm, and she was out the door and into the fresh night air. Kristin was grateful to feel the colder temperatures on her face after being in the stuffy library all day with crowds. More than once she felt lightheaded, and her stomach had turned over off and on, so she counted on the air to revive her a bit.

Kristin got to her car, sat behind the wheel, and started the engine. She rolled the window down so she could feel the breeze on her face as she drove. Before she pulled out, she looked at her cell phone and saw there were a couple of messages. One was from Izzy, and it was a picture of her from rehearsals dressed as a mermaid with a big smile on her face. The shiny green body certainly stood out in the photo.

The second message was from Wes and asked her when she might be home tonight. It had come in a few hours ago, but in all the hubbub at the library, she evidently overlooked it. Kristin told him she would be late tonight, and hopefully this wouldn't cause another situation to argue about. The arguments and brief conversations grew more and more, the closer it came to Opening Day.

The last message was from a phone number she did not recognize. Kristin opened the message to read it:

I hope everything went well at the events today. It looks like you really know what you're doing. I look forward to working with you and our next meeting. Let me know when we can get together.

Richard

"Richard? Who's Richard?" Kristin said out loud to herself. It then dawned on her that it was Richard Trainor, the new board member. She was surprised he bothered to text her after just seeing her this afternoon, but Kristin took it as a positive sign that he genuinely wanted to take part in advancing the library's cause.

Kristin put her phone away and drove home. She pulled past Wyatt and Jenny's and noticed that all the lights were out in their house already. She worried that the same would be true when she got up the hill. A quick glance as she drew in front of the house let her know that Izzy's light was still on. Izzy was probably doing homework or just chatting online with her friends or boyfriend. Now Kristin wondered about Wes.

Kristin slowly opened and closed the front door and worked her way inside the quiet house. She walked through the kitchen and saw no signs of life, and while the lights were on in the bedroom, there was no sign of Wes. Kristin left her bag in the bedroom and moved her way down the steps to the entertainment room. There she saw Wes sitting back on the leather couch, his bare feet up on the ottoman, as he watched a Spring Training game on the television. Kristin tensed, worried it meant he was going to be in a bad mood.

Wes peeked his head up as he heard her footsteps cross into the room.

"Hey, I was wondering when you were going to show," he said to her with a smile.

"Sorry I'm late," Kristin said. She shifted over to the couch and sat next to Wes. "I thought I told you

I was going to be late tonight. We had the author's day at the library today."

"I forgot all about it," Wes said honestly. He watched as Kristin took off her sneakers and put her feet in Wes' lap. Wes started to rub the soles of her feet, massaging away some of the aches.

"Oh, that feels nice," Kristin purred, closing her eyes.

"It's alright," Wes told her as he kept up the foot massage. "I saved a plate for you if you're hungry. I made Salisbury steak."

Kristin peered over at Wes.

"No, my stomach has been in knots all day. I think it's been the stress of today, and, well, everything. Wait a minute, you cooked? You haven't made dinner in weeks."

"Well, I realized I hadn't done a lot of things in weeks," Wes told her. His fingers moved from Kristin's soles to her heels, causing another light moan of pleasure and relaxation.

"It's okay, Wes, I understand…. Ahhhh," Kristin cooed. "If it means you're going to do more of this, we're all good," she said with a smile.

"I know I've been neglecting you, and Izzy, and my parents, and just about everything else, and I know I've said I'm sorry before in the last few weeks, Kris, but I am. I think it's all turning a corner now."

Kristin nodded in agreement and got lost in the feeling from Wes' touch. Besides the arguing, they had hardly spent any intimate moments together in the last few weeks. She noticed Wes' hands had moved up from her feet to her calves, massaging her muscles through her stockings. Before long, Wes had gone higher, pushing Kristin's black linen skirt up so that it was nearly around her waist. Kristin kept her eyes closed, getting more aroused as she enjoyed the feeling.

"I couldn't wait to get home and get these pantyhose and this bra off," Kristin remarked as she felt Wes hook his fingers inside the top of her pantyhose and peel them down her legs. The rush of fresh air she felt on her legs sent chills up her body.

"I think I can oblige you with all that," Wes growled as he crumpled the pantyhose up into a ball and tossed them on the floor. His fingers quickly went to work on the buttons of her white blouse until it was completely undone. His fingers deftly opened the front clasp of her nude-colored bra, freeing her breasts.

Wes moved his body over Kristin's and pressed himself against her as they kissed. Kristin's hands hungrily pulled the t-shirt over Wes' head so she could feel his bare chest against hers. His arousal was as evident as hers now as her fingers shot down to his jeans so she could unbutton and unzip. The jeans were down to his ankles in no time, with a little help from Wes, and Kristin gripped his strengthening erection through his briefs.

It was Wes' turn to groan now, and his mouth first went to the nape of Kristin's neck, kissing her over and over. His body moved against her hand with a will of its own, and Wes noticed that Kristin was shimmying out of her panties, getting them down just enough so that when she freed Wes from his briefs, he easily slipped inside her.

Kristin's initial gasp at the feeling immediately turned to moans of more profound pleasure as the couple moved together now. Kristin kept her eyes closed, lost in the intensity. She heard herself panting loudly, and her fingers gripped the strong, tense muscles in Wes' back as she tried to pull him even closer to her. The friction caused by Wes' chest rubbing against her own nipples made them ultra-sensitive, and each movement felt electric, causing her to suck her breath in.

Wes brought his lips close to Kristin's left ear, kissing her shoulder.

"Kris…" he whispered, "I'm…" Kristin knew by his groans he edged closer.

"Oh God, Wes, yes," she said, wrapping her legs tight around his waist to pull him to her as she lifted her hips off the couch.

That was the only sign Wes needed as his body tensed. His hands gripped Kristin's torso tight as he came, and it was more than enough to push Kristin over the precipice so that she experienced her orgasm as well. She groaned louder than she expected, and she was grateful the volume on the TV was up to cover the noise.

Wes collapsed against Kristin's body, and the two lay together on the couch, trying to catch their breath. Kristin combed her fingers through Wes' hair as his head rested just below her breasts.

"Oh, I have missed that," Kristin said breathlessly. "I need to come home late more often."

They both stayed against one another on the couch for minutes, giving each other light kisses, before Wes sat back.

"Where are you going?" Kristin said, beckoning him to come back.

Wes considered the question and decided that now was not the ideal time to answer that question with the truth, that he planned to go play with the Washington team.

"Nowhere," he said with a smile. "I was just going to pull my pants up in case Izzy came downstairs."

"Hmmm, I hadn't really thought about that," Kristin answered, pulling up her panties and pushing her skirt back down. "I guess I got caught up in the moment." Kristin worked her way out of the unclasped bra and buttoned her shirt up.

"You and me both," Wes smirked as he put his t-shirt back on.

"So, I take it the day at the library went well," Wes asked.

Kristin leaned in as Wes put his arm around her as they sat on the couch now.

"It was great," Kristin said proudly. "We had big crowds, the authors were fantastic, and I heard nothing but good things from all the people I encountered. We will definitely do it again. I think we'll get some excellent attention from the day, and maybe more visitors and more donations."

"That's great Kris," Wes said, giving her a kiss on the cheek. "I'm so proud of you."

Kristin blushed and smiled. "Thank you," she said softly.

"We should celebrate," Wes said, getting up off the couch.

"I thought that's what we just did," Kristin added with a smirk.

Wes walked behind the bar and pulled out two champagne flutes, along with a bottle of champagne that chilled in the fridge. Before Kristin could say anything, Wes popped the cork and mist sprayed up from the bottle, and he began to pour into both glasses.

Wes walked back around and handed a glass to Kristin.

"To the best librarian in the state. And I'm not just saying that because you live here," Wes said as he clinked glasses with Kristin.

Wes took a big slug of champagne, and Kristin sipped hers lightly. She quickly put the glass down on the floor next to the couch, stood up, and raced towards the bathroom.

Before Wes reacted, Kristin slammed the bathroom door closed, flipped up the toilet seat, and vomited. The retching sounds came through loud and clear, and Wes walked over to the door. He gently rapped on the door.

"Kris, are you okay?" Wes asked with concern.

Kristin's stomach cramped once again as she threw up a bit more. She wiped the spittle from her mouth before she lifted her head.

"I'm alright," she said as she attempted to regain her composure.

"Okay," Wes replied, "but it's not a real big ego boost when the woman you just made love to runs into the bathroom to puke," he said jokingly.

Another wave struck Kristin as she got sick again.

"Not funny right now, Wes," she managed to get out.

"Can I get you anything? Do you want me to come in?"

Just then, the toilet flushed. Kristin pulled the door open and stood in front of Wes, her shirt crumpled and covered with a few small stains.

"I don't know if it was not eating right today, too much coffee, or something I picked up from someone at the library. I think the smell of the champagne pushed me over the edge. I'm feeling a little better," Kristin said, wiping her mouth on her bare arm.

"Why don't you go get changed and get to bed? I'll get you a bottle of water. You want some Pepto or something?" Wes asked, trying to help.

"Oh no," Kristin said, holding her stomach. "The smell of that stuff might make it worse."

Kristin worked her way up the stairs while Wes cleaned up downstairs. He dumped out the champagne and straightened up the mussed cushions on the couch before he turned off the TV and went upstairs. He moved to the fridge and grabbed a couple of bottles of water to bring to Kristin. When he got to the bedroom, Kristin was already under the covers, fast asleep.

Wes placed the two bottles of water on the nightstand next to Kristin's side of the bed and gave her a gentle kiss on the forehead as he moved some strands of her blond hair out of her eyes. Kristin gave a small sigh and smile as she snuggled further into her pillow.

Wes removed his jeans and put them, along with Kristin's clothing that was balled up on the floor, into the nearby hamper before he got into bed. He never got the chance to tell Kristin his news of the day, and he knew Randy would be getting back to him with more details tomorrow.

Tomorrow is another day, Wes thought as he picked up his phone so he could read up some more about the Frontier League and the Washington Wild Things.

13

Kristin had awakened twice during the night and got sick, and each time Wes got up with her to make sure she was okay or to clean up afterward. The fitful sleep made it that much harder to get up in the morning, and she had no memory of her alarm going off because either it hadn't, or she slept through it. When Kristin got up and saw the clock showed 11 AM, she flew into a panic and leaped out of bed and raced to the bathroom to turn the shower on. She stripped out of the thin t-shirt she wore, her second of the night, and climbed into the shower even before the water had a chance to warm up. The cold water shocked her system, and Kristin's eyes went wide as she worked through it. She washed her hair and body the best she could to get the stale smell off her that made her nauseated once again.

Kristin shut the shower off and got out to brush her teeth to get the bad taste from her mouth. She walked into the bedroom and removed clothes from her closet and dresser for the day when Wes walked in.

"What are you doing?" he asked her.

"I'm late for work, Wes," Kristin rushed. She grabbed her undergarments out of the top drawer of her dresser and started to dress.

"No, you're not," Wes told her as he took her by the shoulders. "I called Karen this morning and told her you were sick and weren't coming in. You were up half the night, and you obviously have some stomach bug. Go back to bed," he commanded and guided her towards the mattress.

"Wes, I have too much to do. We have to clean up from yesterday, and I have pictures to upload, mail to answer. There's stuff that needs to get done," Kristin protested. She pulled away from Wes to start to dress again.

"Stop being stubborn and listen to me. I'm trying to help you. Just get some rest. All that stuff will still be there tomorrow. I'll call Karen and ask her if she needs help moving anything. I can go down and help her if she does. It will be fine." Wes brought Kristin back to the bed and had her lay down again.

"Okay," Kristin resigned. She got under the covers but propped herself up with some pillows. "Can I at least use my phone to see if Karen needs anything?"

"Sure," Wes said, handing her cell phone to her.

"Do you want anything? Water? Soup? A banana?"

"Some water, please. And a banana," Kristin offered, taking her phone.

Wes went into the kitchen to fetch the items while Kristin looked at her phone. She didn't see any messages at all from Karen or anyone affiliated with the library. The lack of urgency gave her some reassurance. Wes quickly returned to the bedroom with a couple of bottles of water.

"We're all out of bananas," Wes told her. "I'm going to run down to the store to get some. You need anything else?"

"Wes, really, you don't have to..." Kristin started to say before Wes cut her off.

"I'll be back in ten minutes. Text me or call me if you need anything else."

Wes started to walk out of the room.

"Don't I get a kiss goodbye?" Kristin asked.

"I'm not kissing you if you're sick," Wes said, and blew her a kiss and smiled as he left.

As soon as she heard the front door close, Kristin picked up her cell phone and called the library.

"Chandler Public Library," Karen said in a sweet, professional voice.

"Karen, it's me," Kristin told her.

"Hey, Kris. How are you feeling? Wes said you puked your guts out."

"Really? Wes said that?" Kristin said, shocked Wes would say that to anyone.

"Okay, he didn't say it that way, but that was the gist of it," Karen confessed. "What's going on?"

"I guess I have some stomach flu or virus or something, I don't know. Are you okay down there? I can come in if you need help."

"Kris, I'm fine. It's dead in here," Karen responded. "Just a few of the regulars this morning. I was able to get everything cleaned up, and most of it is put back where it belongs. There's nothing important going on down here."

"Oh, okay," Kristin was a bit let down that there wasn't more of a buzz about yesterday. "No one said anything about yesterday and how it went?"

"A few people said they had a good time yesterday, so I think it went well. Marion called looking for you, but she said it was nothing important and that she heard we did well yesterday. That was about it."

"Alright, well I guess I can leave you…" Karen cut Kristin off.

"Oh wait, there was one thing," Karen remarked.

"What? Should I come down?" Kristin said, flipping the blanket off.

"No, but you should know about it," Karen's voice was hushed now. "That Richard Trainor came in again today looking for you. I told him you were home sick and asked if I could help him with anything, but he said no, that he was looking to talk to you. Something about a meeting."

"Yeah, I told him I would meet with him to talk about projects, and funding, and stuff like that. I didn't set up a time or day or anything with him. I guess he's anxious to see what's going on. He texted me last night, too."

"I don't know, Kris, he kind of gives me the creeps. The whole time I felt like he was sizing me up the way he looked at me. He seems a little too friendly." Karen had concern in her voice.

"I didn't get that vibe from him, Karen, honestly. He's just new to town and trying to meet people and get involved. Let's give him a chance. Besides, I think he can be a big help to us."

"Okay, but other than that, nothing is going on here. Get yourself better, and you can come in tomorrow. Just think tomorrow is Friday. You get the chance to relax for the weekend after that. I gotta go; Mrs. Pauling just walked in, and you know how she is if someone is on the phone and she wants help. Talk to you later," Karen said before hanging up.

It seems like everything is under control, Kristin thought. She set her head back into the pillow behind her, unsure of what to do with herself. She did think about what Karen said about Richard Trainor. He did have an avid interest right away, and that could easily be misinterpreted, but Kristin would tuck that information in the back of her mind for now. For the moment, she was going to relax and try to kick this bug.

****

Wes got to the grocery store with the sole mission of finding the bananas and getting out as fast as he could. Even though he had stopped playing pro ball, people in town still liked to stop and chat about his playing days. He appreciated the fans and always tried to be as obliging as he could. He signed autographs, posed for pictures, and listened to stories, but there were days like today where he had things he needed to do.

The trip to the store also would give him more time to figure out what he should say to Kristin about the offer from the Wild Things. He hoped to tell her when she got home yesterday, but they got caught up in passion, and then she was sick, and he didn't want to make things worse for her.

Wes examined the bananas laid out on the table as he tried to figure out which would be the best to get. He didn't do much of the shopping, and even when he did, produce was something he usually left for Kristin or Izzy. Wes had no idea which would be best, though he did know the bunches that were still green were off-limits. He found a group of five that appeared yellow enough and picked them up, only to hear a voice behind him.

"If you were going to eat them today, those aren't the ones you want."

He spun around to see his father Wyatt standing there, pushing a small cart with some groceries.

"Hi, Dad. What's wrong with these?" Wes asked. He held the bananas closer to his face to get a better look at them.

Wyatt sighed at his son and grabbed the bananas. "Look, they're still pretty green towards the stems, and they feel hard. They will not be pleasant for Kristin to eat if she's not feeling good. Take these instead; they're perfect," Wyatt added, picking up a bunch that was yellow and lightly speckled with brown dots.

"Thanks, Dad," Wes chirped. "Wait, how did you know Kris wasn't feeling good? Are you psychic now, too?"

"Sometimes I am, boy," Wyatt smiled. "No, Izzy called me this morning to ask me to pick her up after rehearsal tonight, so you and Kristin didn't have to go out. How's her stomach?"

The two men walked casually towards the front registers.

"She said she's better, but I don't know. She was pretty sick last night and still looked a bit pale this morning. Probably just a virus she picked up. She's burned the candle at both ends pretty hard lately."

Wes placed his bananas on the conveyor belt at the register and waited his turn.

"A lot of stress going on lately too with work and you," Wyatt added, grabbing the plastic bar to separate his order from Wes'.

"What about me? I haven't stressed her out." Wes wanted to believe that was true.

"Really? You don't think so? Come on, Wes. You've been ornery on and off for weeks with all this baseball stuff, and she knows you've been keeping stuff from her. How do you think it makes her feel?"

Wyatt finished putting all the vegetables he was buying and a pint of coffee toffee bar ice cream on the belt. Wes took a quick look down and then smiled at his father.

"Who's the ice cream for? I'm pretty sure Mom doesn't eat it, and you're not supposed to have any. Now, who's keeping things from people?"

"Mind your business, boy. It's your turn to pay," Wyatt scolded as he pointed at the cashier.

Wes paid for his bananas and waited for his father to finish his purchase so they could walk out together. They stopped next to Wyatt's truck, and Wyatt loaded his bags on the passenger seat.

"Dad, I have to let you know something," Wes started. "I got an offer yesterday, and I'm going to take it."

Wyatt turned to his son and tipped his Stetson hat back on his head.

"What team?" Wyatt questioned.

"Well, that's just it," Wes began. "It's with the Washington Wild Things."

Wes could see the wrinkles on his father's forehead as Wyatt thought about what his son had said. Wyatt's eyes went wide when he figured it out.

"That independent team a few towns over? Why… why would you want to do that, Wes?"

"Because it's a chance to play, Dad. If I do well enough, maybe some big-league team will pick me up during the season, and I could get another chance."

Wes' feet shifted beneath him like he did when he was telling things to his father when he was a boy and knew his Dad would disapprove.

"That's a pretty tall order, Wes. And what if it doesn't work out? Suppose no one picks you up, or you don't play well. What then? And what about Izzy and Kristin? Where are they in all this? Do they know?"

"I have to take the chance, Dad," Wes said as he tried to convince his father it was the right move. "If I don't at least try, I will always wonder if it was the right thing to do. If I try and fail, so be it, but at least I will have tried. As for Kristin and Izzy… no, I haven't told them yet."

"What are you waiting for?" Wyatt leaned back on his truck now for support.

"I don't know, but it… it has to be today. I have to go to the team on Sunday to start practice. Randy just texted me this morning," Wes confessed.

"Jesus, Wes," Wyatt shook his head and gave a sideways glance to his son. He saw that Wes was torn about it and needed some fatherly advice and support.

"Look, you know your Mom and I will do whatever we can to help out with Izzy. We always have. And Kristin… well, she's family to us too, and I would hate to think that this was going to come between all that…"

"Nothing's going to change, Dad," Wes interrupted. "The team is just as close as the mall. When they are at home, I'll be able to stay here at the house with everyone so it will be just like always. When I'm on the road, I'll be gone for a week or two at a time and then be back. It will better than when I was playing for Pittsburgh and was gone for months. It will all work out, I promise."

"Okay," Wyatt told him, patting him on the shoulder. "You better get home and make sure Kristin is feeling alright. Just let me know if you need help with anything."

"Thanks, Dad. I appreciate it. I'll talk to you later."

Wes walked towards his truck, knowing his father watched him as he did. The pit of Wes' stomach burned now, and not because he was getting sick too. He worried even more about talking to Kristin about his plans and how she would react.

Wes' ride home was consumed with how he would break the news to Kristin and Izzy. Every scenario he came up with seemed to have it end badly, no matter how much he didn't want it to be that way.

Wes' entered the house and heard the tea kettle whistling loudly. He walked into the kitchen and saw the steam rising rapidly from the pot with no one in sight. He turned the gas off, so the kettle quieted down and went into the bedroom to see Kristin come out of the bathroom, wiping her mouth.

"You okay?" Wes asked, looking into her eyes.

"I think so," Kristin rasped. "I thought I would make some tea and started the teapot going. I noticed the orange juice still out on the counter, so I went to put it away, but as soon as I opened the fridge, I got hit with a whiff of something that made my stomach jump. I had to run into the bathroom right away."

"It was probably Izzy's leftovers from last night. She and her friends went to the diner, and she had the fried chicken and garlic mashed potatoes…"

Kristin held up her hand to Wes.

"Wes, stop," she begged. "Just hearing about it is making me smell it again."

"Do you want me to fix the tea for you?" Wes asked gently.

"Please," Kristin said as she climbed back into bed.

Wes prepared a mug of tea and placed an unpeeled banana on the tray next to the cup and brought it to Kristin.

"Here, in case you feel up to having something later," Wes offered.

"Thanks," Kristin smiled. "You're my hero."

Pangs of guilt flushed through Wes' system at her words.

"Kris, there's something I have to tell you," Wes said, taking her hand in his. Kristin turned and looked right into Wes' eyes.

"I... I heard from Randy yesterday," he started. "I didn't get a chance to tell you last night with everything... everything that went on."

Kristin let out a light giggle, thinking back to their interlude, and then made her face serious again as she could see Wes had something important to say.

"There's a team that wants me to come to play for them," Wes said, getting it out as fast as he could. Wes saw that Kristin almost held her breath now.

"What... what team?" she said softly, a knot tightening in her stomach now.

"Well, that's the good part... there's an independent team in Washington that's interested."

"D.C. or Washington the state?" she questioned. "Either way, it's not really close by Wes."

"No, Washington, Pennsylvania, not more than a half-hour from here, right near the mall. The Washington Wild Things. You might not have ever heard of them if you don't follow baseball, they are a small..."

Wes looked up to see Kristin's eyes clouding over.

"Kris, I know this isn't what we planned or talked about, but it gives me a chance."

"Wes, we never talked or planned about any of it," Kristin chided. "You did all the planning without ever letting me in on it. We should at least talk about it before you decide anything, don't you think?"

"I… I already gave them an answer," Wes confessed.

"I see." Kristin turned her head to break eye contact with Wes. "Well, at least you'll be at home every day until the season starts, so it gives us time to adjust to everything."

Kristin grabbed a tissue and wiped her eyes and nose. "When is the first day?"

"That's another thing," Wes said. Each statement seemed to make things go more poorly, and Wes knew a worse reaction lay around the corner. "You see, practice starts Sunday and I'll… I'll have to stay with the team in Washington until the season begins in May. I booked a room at the Ramada there this morning."

Silence hung in the air between the two. Wes uncomfortably fidgeted on the bed and stared at Kristin. He wished she would say something, but nothing came.

"Kris? Say something," Wes pleaded.

"What do you want me to say, Wes? You obviously have it all under control and figured out; what do you need me for? You… you should probably think about how much you are going to have to pack and what you want to bring, and maybe work out with your parents about Izzy. She'll need rides and maybe to stay down there with them."

Kristin climbed out of bed without a thought about how much her stomach tumbled.

"Kris, get back in bed. You're still not feeling great. We have today and tomorrow to work all those things out, and besides, you'll be here so Izzy can just stay here until you get home, and my Dad said they would help out and pick her up from rehearsals…"

"You… you already talked to your father about it?" Kristin broke down now. "You told your Dad before you said anything to me?"

"I… it just came up in conversation this morning. I didn't even think about it," Wes fumbled for the right thing to say, but it never came.

"Right, you didn't even think about it, or me," Kristin said as she nodded and sniffled back tears. She stripped off her pajamas and threw on the pants and blouse she had taken out to wear to work this morning.

"What are you doing?" Wes said as he watched Kristin pace the room, collect items, and stuff them in the bag she grabbed from the closet.

"I'm going to work, and then I am going to stay with Karen," Kristin yelled. "Do what you need to do, Wes. I won't get in your way."

"Kris, stop," Wes said as he grabbed her wrist that held her bag. "Let's talk about this."

"We had plenty of time to talk about it for the last few weeks, and you never wanted to, Wes. The time for talking passed long ago. I need to figure stuff out now, and I can't do that here."

Kristin pulled her arm away and raced out of the house. She pulled out her keys so she could get into her Jeep. She tore down the hill and out onto Route 5 so she could get into Chandler and to the library, leaving Wes standing at the front door to watch as she left.

14

Wes spent the better part of Friday and Saturday trying to get Kristin to see him or talk to him. He went to the library, but she stayed in her office and would not come out while he was there. Phone calls and text messages proved useless, and when he showed up at Karen's house, where Kristin stayed, for now, it seemed pointless, though once she yelled at him out of a window that she would call the police if he continued to sit and wait outside Karen's house.

When Sunday morning arrived, Wes knew he had to choose between staying or leaving. All the clothing and equipment he thought he would need was loaded into the back of his truck since Saturday, but as 1 PM inched closer on Sunday and Wes knew he would have to go, he readied to unpack. It was then Wes saw his father's pickup amble up the hill and stop just in front of Wes' vehicle. He clearly made out his father's cowboy hat silhouette in the car, but then he also saw Kristin seated next to him.

His father got out and slowly walked over to the passenger side of his truck to open the door for Kristin, who slipped out of the truck, clad in a t-shirt and jeans. Wes walked quickly over to Kristin and took her hands.

"Kris, thank God you are here. I'm going to…" Kristin put a finger up to Wes' lips to quiet him.

"Wes, let me talk," Kristin told him. "Look, I'm not happy about how all this played out and how you didn't let me in on what you were planning or anything…"

"Kris, I…"

Kristin shushed him again.

"I'm angry about it, Wes, but more than angry, I'm disappointed, and I'm hurt. It's going to take me a while to get over that and get through it. I know playing again is important to you, and if you had given us the chance to talk about it, I think you would have found out that I support you. It's going to take some thought to sort things out, but that doesn't mean I won't be here for Izzy or your parents. I'll help out with whatever they need me for while you are gone."

Wes sighed in relief and went to retake Kristin's hands, but she pulled them away.

"But I thought…" Wes stated, confusedly.

"It doesn't mean we're completely okay, Wes," Kristin told him. "I think we can both use this time apart to evaluate our relationship."

Kristin leaned over and gave Wes a long kiss on the cheek and then kissed his lips softly.

"I still love you, Wes Martin. Good luck," she whispered, choking back tears.

"Kris, wait!" Wes yelled as she walked back to the truck and got in.

Wes took a few steps towards the truck before his father moved in front of him to hold him back. Wyatt turned Wes around and started walking him back towards Wes' house.

"Son, you need to give her some space right now," Wyatt told him. "It took a lot just to convince her to come here. Your mother, Izzy and I talked to her at different points yesterday and today to let her know how important she is to all of us."

"Dad, I'm not going to go, this is crazy. I'll call Randy and end this," Wes said and pulled out his cell phone.

"You think that's the answer?" Wyatt said crossly. "And then what? We go through all this again next year when you feel the same way? It's not fair to anyone, Wes, to do that. Go to Washington and start training with the team. You need to see for certain if it is what you want and how it plays out."

"But what about Kristin?" Wes said, looking back at his father's truck. He could see Kristin looked back at him.

"It's in her hands, Wes. She has to decide what's best for her, just like you do. She'll be around us, and you know I'll watch out for her, but she's a strong woman. She can take care of herself. Let Kristin be so she can figure it out for herself. It's the best thing for all involved right now."

"I'm not giving up on her, Dad," Wes told his father. "I'M NOT GIVING UP ON YOU!!" Wes yelled back to the truck.

"Come on, son," Wyatt said, guiding Wes to Wes' truck. "Good luck. You know we're all rooting for you."

"Just let me know she's alright, Dad," Wes asked as he closed the door.

"I will don't worry. It's only a month until the season starts, right?"

"Yeah, but we start on the road. The first home game is May 17th."

"We'll be there for sure," Wyatt reassured.

Wes shook his head as he started his truck. He pulled slowly down the driveway hill, moving to the side and onto the grass so he could drive passed his father's truck. He stopped his truck next to Wyatt's and rolled down his window. Kristin didn't roll down her window but did turn to look at him.

"You know I love you. I'll be back, I promise," Wes said loud enough so Kristin could hear him. She was still crying and showed no other reaction, though Wes thought for sure he saw her nod her head as he pulled away.

****

The short ride to Washington was one that Wes took thousands of times over the years, but never one he made to go and play ball. The stadium in the town, Consol Energy Park, opened back in 2002 when Wes began his minor league career with the Pirates. The family went to the mall at Washington Crown Center often, but they never ventured a little further down the road to the stadium.

Wes got off I-70 and headed towards the Ramada to get to his room before the trip over to the stadium. He pulled off the highway and found the hotel quickly, a pleasant-looking place perched high atop a hill so that visitors enjoyed a magnificent view of the area. Wes pulled his truck into an available spot near the door, grabbed his clothing bag, and went inside.

The hotel itself was old-school, the design right out of the 50s or 60s when every place had dark wood all over. A quick glance at the bar let Wes know that is precisely how the décor was everywhere. The woman who checked him in, by the name of Cathy, was pleasant and friendly and didn't give the slightest bit of recognition to who he was or why he might be there. She was happy to see he would be staying with them for so long, and she let Wes know about the breakfast buffet in the mornings and the hours of the restaurant and bar and wished him a good day before she moved on to the family that came in behind him so they could get accommodations.

The room, like the rest of the hotel, was an older design, but sitting on the king-sized mattress let him know the bed provided the comfort he needed each night. Wes put his clothing and toiletries away so that it would feel a bit more like he was living there for the next month before he headed out of the room and over to the stadium.

The stadium sat a stone's throw away from the hotel, a short ride down I-70 past the mall. Wes pulled into the stadium parking, unsure of where he should go. He walked around the stadium to different locations, and he spotted some people out grooming the field, and a few players in uniforms already on the field looking things over and stretching.

A tap on his shoulder jolted Wes, and he spun around to see who it was. A woman stood before him, dressed in a red polo shirt with the team logo on the left chest, what looked like a mountain lion wearing sunglasses and smiling/growling. Wes' eyes locked onto hers, a dark brown that made it hard not to notice them.

"Are you Wes? Wes Martin?" she asked with a smile.

"Yes, I am," he said sheepishly, wondering if she was just a fan.

"Hi, Wes. I'm Sabrina Watkins. I take care of media relations and PR for the Wild Things. It's nice to meet you."

Sabrina held her delicate hand out to Wes, and he took it in his. She had a much firmer grip than he thought she would before she moved her hand away.

"I'm sorry if I startled you, but I've been waiting for you to get here. We just need you to come into the office first to sign your contract and all, and then we do have some media present that may want to ask some questions and such before we get you into your uniform. Sound good?"

"Yeah, of course," Wes answered. "I'm sorry if I'm a little late. Randy… my agent… didn't really tell me what time to get here."

"No worries," she said, smiling again. This time her eyes roamed up and down Wes' body. "You'll find we're pretty laid back here, though we are very excited to have you with the team."

Wes followed Sabrina through one of the outer doors and down a hallway to where a few of the offices were located. Sabrina led him to the office of the General Manager, noticeable by the large plaque on the door. Sabrina knocked on the door before they entered. The man behind the desk smiled as Wes and Sabrina came into the room. He stood up to shake Wes' hand.

"Wes, hi, I'm Tom Killian. I'm the President and General Manager of the Wild Things. It's great to have you here."

"Nice to meet you, Tom," Wes said. The office was small, perhaps smaller than what Wes thought the president of a team would have, and Tom, with his short hair, and blue eyes, looked like he was just barely out of college. Wes suddenly felt ancient as he stood there and wondered if this was all a mistake.

"You two have stuff to work out," Sabrina offered. "Tom, give me a call when you are done so we can get Wes down in front of the media."

"Have a seat, Wes," Tom pointed to one of the chairs opposite his desk. "Can I get you anything? Water or soda?" Tom opened the mini-fridge in the corner of his office.

"No, thanks, Tom," Wes answered politely.

"Okay, then let's get down to it." Tom sat down at his desk and pulled out paperwork. It was Wes' contract.

"I already sent this over to your agent… nice guy by the way. I don't deal with too many agents, really. Most players have their parents or just themselves when they do this."

When Tom said "parents," Wes barely stifled a cringe.

"It's pretty standard, and Randy didn't see any problems with it," Tom pointed out. "Now, the salary… well, it's a lot less than what you are used to I'm sure, but that's standard pay for our team. I didn't really have the budget to give you more, but there will be promotional opportunities that come up in the area. I am sure you can make some extra money if you want. A lot of the guys on the team do it."

Wes glanced at the line noting the salary of $725 a month. The last contract he had signed with the Pirates a few years ago paid him millions, but this wasn't about the money.

"I'm not really worried about the salary, Tom," Wes stated as he flipped to the last page of the contract. "It's not about the money for me. I just want to play." Wes grabbed the pen and scrawled his signature on the appropriate lines.

"Fantastic!" Tom shouted. "I'll send a copy of this to Randy, and we are good to go. Let's get you to

Sabrina for the press stuff and then you can meet the team. Most of the guys are here already."

Wes and Tom walked down the hall two offices to where Sabrina was. She reclined in her chair while on the phone with someone with her feet crossed on her desk, giving both gentlemen a view of her toned legs in the short skirt she was wearing.

"We're all done, Sabrina," Tom told her. "He's all yours. See you later, Wes. Welcome to the team!" Tom vigorously slapped Wes on the back and left the office. Wes' gaze shifted back to Sabrina, who now perched herself right in front of him again.

"Okay, let's get you into your jersey before we head down," Sabrina said, bending over at the waist to grab the jersey off the chair behind her. She spun back around to face Wes.

"Can you take your jacket off?" she asked sweetly.

Wes unzipped the leather jacket he always wore and placed it down on one of the other chairs in the room. He was wearing just a plain black t-shirt underneath.

"Nice," Sabrina muttered. "You've kept yourself in good shape, huh?" Sabrina eyed Wes' biceps as she spoke.

"I tried," Wes replied, holding out his hands to take the maroon-colored jersey from her. Wes flipped it over to see his name on the back arched over the familiar number 12 he wore for most of his life.

"Number 12 is correct, right?" Sabrina asked. "I tried to do my homework on you before you got here for the press release."

"Yes, 12 is perfect," Wes said, pulling the jersey on and loving the familiar feeling that washed over him.

Sabrina reached over and started buttoning the front of the jersey for Wes.

"We have just a few media people downstairs… local newspaper and TV, local radio, and some Pittsburgh reporters to branch things out. We'll also be broadcasting live on our social media so everyone can see you."

When she completed buttoning the jersey, her hands lingered on Wes' pecs before Wes took a step back.

"Looks great," Sabrina added. "I think we're all set. Follow me."

Wes walked behind Sabrina as they made their way down the hall and took a left that led them out to where the ball field was. It was challenging to keep his eyes off Sabrina, who was purposefully swaying her hips a bit more to draw Wes' attention. Warmth and discomfort crept into Wes' body, and he gladly stepped out onto the field, where things were open and airy, and the small group of reporters had gathered.

Tom was already out on the field talking to reporters and invited Wes over to join him in front of home plate so he could introduce him. Wes scanned and saw a couple of TV cameras among the reporters, and there were a few people from Pittsburgh newspapers that he recognized from his time in the majors. Tom gave a brief introduction about how glad they were to have Wes as part of the team and then gave Wes the floor to answer questions.

Wes got peppered with questions about why now for a comeback, why it wasn't with a major league team, and others that put him off, but he kept up a brave front. He gave all the answers he could about how he just wanted to play hard for Washington and how grateful he was to get a chance to play a bit and maybe pass some wisdom on to younger players, and all the other 'party line' answers other players in his position gave over the years.

Once all of the questions finished, Wes posed for a few more pictures with Tom and some with a bat in his hands, and then the event ended. The reporters dispersed, Tom headed back inside, and Wes was left standing there with Sabrina. Wes turned and looked towards the outfield and saw a few players out there having a catch that watched the spectacle unfold.

Glad to have the presentation completed, Wes stood at home plate and wondered what to do next.

"Okay, that's it," Sabrina told him.

"Now what?" Wes asked.

"I'll get you inside, so you go to the locker room, get changed, and get started. The rest of the team will be out here to practice in a bit, so you should go down and meet John Clines, our manager, and talk things over."

Once again, Wes trailed behind Sabrina uncomfortably. They went through the dugout and down the tunnel to the locker room door. Sabrina made no bones about her bravado and walked right in and headed straight for the manager's office. There were players in there in various states of dress and undress, which didn't faze Sabrina one bit.

"Don't be shy boys," she said with a laugh. "You don't have anything I haven't seen before." She turned to Wes and gave him a wink.

Sabrina rapped on the glass of the manager's office door and let herself in. John Clines was in there going over some statistics on his computer screen.

"John Clines, Wes Martin," she said as she introduced the two men. John was just another person who was younger than Wes but only by a year. He was balding early, something typical of ballplayers that wore hats and helmets all the time, and Wes could see that while John once may have been in playing shape, he had a bit of a paunch now that sagged over his baseball pants.

"Nice to meet you, John," Wes offered as they shook hands.

John simply nodded and then looked passed Wes to Sabrina, wrinkling his brow at her.

"Well, that's my cue to leave," Sabrina said. "Wes, it was nice to meet you. If you need anything or have any questions, feel free to contact me. I'll leave a binder with all the team information and everything else on the chair by your locker."

"Thanks, Sabrina," Wes said with a smile.

"My pleasure, Wes," she grinned and gave a light wave before walking out.

Wes pivoted back towards John, who was now seated at his desk again.

"Have a seat, Wes," John told him, pointing to the chair next to the desk.

"I have to say, I was a little surprised when Tom told me that we were signing you. We're only allowed a couple of veteran guys on the team and your age... well, it goes beyond the normal league rules."

John looked over at Wes, giving Wes a stare that let him know he thought Wes received favored treatment.

"John, I realize the situation and how it looks. I didn't pull any strings or anything. Heck, I didn't even know there was a team up here, to be honest. I only want somewhere to play, and this was close to home, so we gave it a shot."

"I get it, Wes. You're taking one last shot at the brass ring and hope a team spots you and picks you up. You don't have to snow me. I know we weren't on your radar, but we were the only team willing to take a flyer on you. I have to tell you I'm not thrilled about it. I'm used to working with kids – guys between 19 and 25 at most – who just want to play. You're taking the spot of someone who has a dream of where you have already been. Tom has all these grand visions of filling ballparks all over because of you, and maybe that will happen, but know this – you're no different than one of the kids. You want to play here, you have to earn it."

"I don't want or expect special treatment, John," Wes explained. "You're the boss here. You decide who plays where and when. Just tell me what to do, and I'll do it. I want to show I can still hit and play. The rest is up to you. Maybe some of the kids can learn a few things while I'm here. I know you guys don't have a hitting coach. I'm happy to help if I can while I'm here."

"Don't go butting your nose in unless someone asks for help. That's all I'm saying," John shot back. "This is my team. Go suit up, and I'll see you out on the field."

"You got it, Skip," Wes said and left the office. He looked around and saw some players still dressing, while others watched him. Wes walked to the locker with his nameplate above it. Wes hadn't seen lockers this small in many years, but if he had a place to change, it was all good. He undressed and put the rest of his uniform on, taking care to make sure his belt was on right, his shirt tucked, and his sanitary socks were straight. Wes heard a couple of snickers from players that moved past him as they went out to the field.

"What is he, a hundred?" one player thundered as those around him laughed.

Wes sat back in his chair, grabbed his glove from his duffel bag, and sighed.

It's going to be a long month, he thought.

15

March rolled into April without much fanfare in Chandler, and signs of spring were popping up everywhere Kristin looked. Flowers and trees budded as she walked along the streets with Karen from Karen's home to the library. Kristin spent a few nights a week with Karen, who thankfully offered up the spare bedroom she had in her home, and then spent other days into the weekend with Izzy so that Karen could have privacy with Brian. It was odd to Kristin every time she set foot in Wes' house, and he wasn't there. She considered it like she was intruding or trespassing in the space, even though Izzy went out of her way to make her feel at home and comfortable.

The two would spend the weekends together when Izzy didn't have to be at rehearsals, and during those times it was not unusual for Kristin to be with Wyatt and Jenny for meals or just to spend time together as she had done before all the turmoil with Wes started. No one would bring up Wes' name, not Izzy or Wyatt or Jenny unless Kristin mentioned him first, and even then, an unease hung in the air that made people hold back.

Wes reached out to Kristin several times, especially in the first few days he was away. He called frequently, but Kristin didn't pick up the phone. He sent text messages, and Kristin occasionally answered those back just to let him know she was okay and getting by. In her heart, she knew it was still too painful to speak to him, and Kristin wasn't over how hurt she felt just yet. She let him know that in the texts she sent him, and eventually, Wes stopped calling and dashed off a text every evening to keep Kristin aware that he thought of her and let her know how he fared with training and practice.

On this Friday morning, while Karen and Kristin walked to the library, they talked about all the final plans Karen made for her wedding. The wedding date laid just about a month away, and she and Brian made deposits to caterers, the DJ, the dress, decorations and more. The two made their way passed Harding's Diner, where Clyde Stuart and his cronies ate their usual breakfast and entertained the morning debates over what appeared in the news that day. Just as the ladies went beyond the window and waved, Clyde hustled out the door.

"Kristin!" Clyde yelled to her.

Kristin turned and smiled at Clyde.

"Yes, Mr. Stuart?"

"Can you settle an argument I'm having with the boys in there?"

"I can try," she told him. "Depends on what you're talking about."

"Well, there's an article in the sports section today about Wes," Clyde told her. Clyde flipped to the page where the small article in the Observer-Reporter, the local newspaper, resided. The title of the article read, 'Is Martin's Run in Washington Over Already?'

"Now, the article says he's having a tough time with the practices up there and all, and the manager is quoted as saying there are no guarantees for anyone, but I'm not buying that bull," Clyde said as he shuffled the pages of the paper closed. "The guys say he's done. Now you must know the truth."

Kristin took a deep breath.

"Mr. Stuart, honestly, I don't know anything about what Wes is doing there or how he's performing. I know he's still there with the team. Beyond that, I couldn't say."

"What?" Clyde crowed. "That's hogwash! You live with the man for crying out loud. Surely you…"

Karen stepped in and cut him off.

"Clyde, she said she doesn't know anything," Karen clipped. "Just leave it at that. You guys are worse than a bunch of old hens. Find something else to debate about."

Karen grabbed Kristin's right arm and hooked her left through it and led the two of them to march down the street and leave Clyde Stuart on the sidewalk with his jaw down.

"Thanks, Karen," Kristin told her.

"No problem," Karen replied. "That old coot needs something better to do."

The two walked along until they reached the library. While Kristin unlocked the door, Karen picked up the conversation again.

"You know, I read that article this morning while you showered, Kris," Karen admitted. "Do you really not know what's going on?"

"Karen, not you too," Kristin said with exasperation. She shut the alarm off and switched the lights on before she moved towards her office.

"It's just that the article says he's struggling pretty badly hitting and fielding, that maybe his ankle isn't holding up. The manager wasn't too optimistic about Wes. Is it that bad?"

Kristin faced Karen while she turned her computer on.

"All I know is from the texts I get from him, Karen. Wes says he's okay and he's trying, and that… well and that's about it. He hurt his ankle back in February. Maybe it's bothering him again. I don't know."

"You never talk on the phone? Or answer his texts? It's been weeks Kris."

Kristin sat down at her desk and shook her head.

"I can't, Karen," Kristin admitted. "I do answer some of the texts, and I try to encourage him, but I can't talk to him on the phone… not yet. I'm not ready."

"I'm not trying to pressure you into anything Kris, you know that," Karen replied. "I just want to make sure you are okay with everything that's going on."

"The less people bring it up, the more okay with it I am," Kristin admitted.

"Fair enough. I'll leave you to your work."

Kristin threw herself into work with abandon, as she had done since Wes left town. Now that she had an ally on the board in Richard Trainor, Kristin had someone to back up her ideas and help sway the board to be more favorable to try new things. She convinced them that it was an excellent way to spend time if they applied for more grant money to get funding for upgrades and improvements. Richard wholeheartedly endorsed many of the programs Kristin pushed for to bring in more speakers, advance reading programs, and expand the genres and sections to have more diversity included, something the board always nixed whenever Kristin brought it up in the past.

Kristin worked diligently on one of the grant proposals when she heard a yell from the library.

"Fuck!" Karen screamed.

Kristin shot out of her office, afraid someone injured themselves, or something fell.

"What's wrong?" Kristin exclaimed. "Are you okay?"

"No, I'm not okay," Karen yelled. The few patrons in the library at the moment all watched with anticipation to see what was going on.

"What's wrong?"

"The hall is what's wrong. They just backed out on the wedding. They said they overlooked another event that had previously been booked for that day. That's total bullshit, Kris. I had them double-check everything before we picked the date. My wedding is ruined. Fuck!"

"Okay, let's go in my office, and you can curse all you want," Kristin said quietly, as she ushered Karen into the room and closed the door.

"Maybe you can talk to them and try to fix it," Kristin said as she tried to calm Karen down.

"Oh, I'm going to talk to them alright," Karen said. "I'm going to kick that bitch Sondra Benning in the teeth. She's the one who was supposed to arrange everything. She's had a beef with me ever since I stole her boyfriend in high school."

Karen stood up, ready to go down and pick a fight.

"Maybe that's not the best approach," Kristin said rationally. "How about you call them first? You can use my phone. I'll go man the front desk."

Kristin stepped out into the library, with people still staring at the door.

"She's fine, really," Kristin stated as she tried to smooth things over. "Just the wedding jitters and all."

"You stuck-up, snotty bitch! I am going to come down there…" Karen could be heard shouting through the office door until Kristin flipped the fan on behind the front desk to drown the noise out.

"Boy, spring has really kicked in around here, hasn't it?" Kristin remarked, fanning herself with a magazine. "Warmest day so far, I think."

A moment later, Karen emerged from Kristin's office, her hair a bit disheveled from all the yelling she did.

"Well," Karen said calmly, "we won't be having the wedding at the Veteran's Hall, and I'm pretty sure I'll never be allowed back in that building again. Kris, what am I going to do? We already gave deposits to save that date. We can't afford to just lose out on all that money and move things around. No one had other times free until the fall."

Karen laid her head on the counter and began to sob. Kristin never saw Karen like that before. Karen was always the strong one that fought through anything.

Kristin consoled Karen as best she could. She rubbed Karen's back and hugged her before Kristin perked up.

"Karen, you had the date of May 22nd, right?"

"Yeah," she said through jagged sobs.

"That's a Friday, right?"

Karen lifted her head up.

"Kris, you're the maid of honor; you're supposed to know all this already. Yes, it's a Friday. So what?"

"I think I figured out what you can do for your wedding, you won't have to change the date, cancel anything, or lose any money."

"We're going to go stuff Sondra in the trunk of my car and dump her in the Allegheny?" Karen asked, hopefully.

"Um, no. We don't need to commit any crimes to make it happen," Kristin assured her. "Let me make a few phone calls and see what I can work out."

Kristin strode into her office with great ideas in her head.

"I am on fire today!" she exclaimed as she picked up the phone.

16

Every day Wes went out to the stadium with the hope that practice would go better than the day before, and every night he returned tired, covered in sweat, and discouraged by what occurred. Even though he had years of pro ball experience facing competition at a higher level, he struggled badly against players much younger than him, including a couple of eighteen-year-olds that were literally half his age. No part of his game went well so far. His fielding suffered greatly from months without practice, and he had a hard time making plays that were routine for him in the past. His hitting that had come along nicely in the batting cages at home now appeared nowhere near that anymore, and he struggled against curveballs and off-speed pitches that came his way. It reached the point where John Clines gave him fewer and fewer reps in the cage and on the field as it got closer and closer to the first game.

Wes fully expected to be cut, but the day never came. Tom Killian pressed John to keep Wes and insisted Wes make the squad because of how good it might look for promotions. Tom already had replica jerseys made with Wes' name and number, he bought 10,000 bobblehead dolls in Wes' likeness and had a half-dozen other ideas he wanted to use for the season. Tom also pressed Wes into service more than once already to meet with potential advertisers to sway them to buy time or billboards on the outfield walls. He even had Sabrina escort Wes around to different places for autograph signings and appearances at everything from schools to car dealerships.

All the treatment had Wes feeling like he was one of the prized horses on his Dad's farm, just there for show and stud and not much else. On the last day of practice, at the end of April when final cuts happened, Wes sat at his locker and slowly packed his things as he waited to get called into John's office to be told he was letting him go. It would be the final indignity, getting sent off to the glue factory.

Gus Jenkins, a twenty-three old outfielder, stormed out of John Clines' office and slammed the door behind him. He flipped over two hampers of towels on his way back to his locker, and a few players went over to ask what happened.

"What's wrong is I'm getting sent packing while Old Man Martin gets to stay on the team, that's what wrong!" Jenkins screamed as he stuffed his belongings in a duffel bag. Gus marched over and stood in front of Wes.

"Have a great night of sleep at the Ramada tonight, Martin," Jenkins yelled. "I get to go back to my host family, get my things, and figure out how I am going to pay my way to get back to Oklahoma where my family is. I hope that extra $725 you get each month makes a difference to you."

"Gus, look," Wes said, as he tried to reason with him. "I'm sorry, but that's not my call. I don't decide on the roster or anything."

"Just save it, okay? It doesn't matter what you say at this point. I got my walking papers."

Gus grabbed his bag and stormed out of the locker room, leaving everyone there to stare at Wes. John Clines walked out of his office to see what was going on.

"Martin, in my office," John barked.

Wes strode into the manager's office, unsure of what to expect.

"Look, John, I don't deserve the spot, and we both know it. Give it to Jenkins," Wes stated.

"Very magnanimous of you, Martin, but there are two problems with that. Number one, Killian would fire me ten minutes after he found out I cut you. Number two, Allen Gentry, who was going to be our back up first baseman, left the club. His father is ill, and his family needed him to come back home. If it weren't for that, it would have been you leaving, trust me, even if Killian did fire me. Killian may make me keep you for now, but he can't make me play you, and you haven't earned it. I hope you're ready to be on the bench a lot. Pinch-hitting and the occasional DH spot is about it for you. Welcome to the team. We leave for Missouri on Sunday. Be here for the bus at 6 AM."

John opened his office door, so Wes could leave. Most of the other players scattered off by the time he got out, all going back to their host family homes. Wes discovered early on that he was the only one on the team staying at a hotel because he was the only one who could afford it. Wes stripped out of his uniform, and tossed it into his locker angrily, and sat down.

"You okay?" a voice said from behind him.

Wes turned to see Emil Stanton standing there. Emil, the left fielder on the team, had the most talent of all the young players. Even though Emil was just twenty, Wes knew Emil had all the tools. Wes saw it enough in the past to know when a player stood out. Emil had the bad luck of getting hurt his senior year in college, so no team wanted to take a chance drafting him.

"Yeah, I'm okay. It's just been… well, it's been a long year, I guess," Wes lamented.

"I hear you," Emil nodded. "I didn't ever think I'd recover from my knee injury last year, but you know what? You inspired me."

"Me?" Wes questioned. "How did I inspire you?"

"When you got cut last spring by the Pirates after you struggled following your knee surgery, you still came back and set that home run record with the Reds. Damn, that was some couple of games you had. After that, I knew I had to keep going too. I worked extra hard, and even though I didn't get drafted, I came here and now, here I am."

"You didn't make it because of me, Emil," Wes told him. "You made it because you're good, really good. You outclass everyone here by a mile. You won't be here long. Scouts will see you play and they'll come calling. Just watch."

"Thanks, man," Emil said, smiling proudly. "You know, I saw you play a bunch of times. My family went to a ton of Pirates games."

"Oh yeah?" Wes said as he pulled on a clean t-shirt.

"Yeah, I think the first time I saw you play I was about seven…"

Wes cut Emil off.

"I don't need to hear anymore, Emil, thanks. You guys already make me feel like I'm 75. But thanks for saying that. It was nice of you."

Emil laughed heartily.

"Okay, man. You have a great night," Emil said, slapping hands with Wes.

"You, too, Emil."

Wes returned to getting dressed, and Emil popped back into the locker room right as Wes tied his sneakers.

"Hey, if you aren't doing anything, do you want to grab some dinner?" Emil asked Wes.

"Gee, I thought about going back to my hotel room to drown my sorrows and watch TV, but, sure, I could eat," Wes said.

"Awesome," Emil said. "I'd love to ask you some questions, if you don't mind, I mean. I think if I worked on my swing some more, maybe I'll get a little more pop, hit some more line drives."

"You bet. I'd be happy to help. I think there's a nice bar nearby with some good burgers and wings and some beers. Let's go there. I'll drive."

"Great, but… well, I won't be drinking," Emil answered as they walked out of the locker room.

"Oh, sure, there's a game coming up in two days. I get it," Wes answered.

"No, man, I'm only twenty," Emil told him. "They'll ID me, and that's it."

Wes groaned.

"Never mind, Emil," Wes told him as he slapped Emil's shoulder. "I still know a place we can go to get some food."

"Alright," Emil said excitedly. "You're buying, right? We haven't gotten a paycheck yet."

17

"This will be perfect," Kristin said to Karen enthusiastically as they walked through the barn corridor. "We can get it decorated all pretty with some strings of lights, and there's plenty of room for all the tables you need, and a dance floor and the DJ. And over here…"

Kristin walked out of the open barn doors to a large grassy area that overlooked the expanse of the farm. "We can put a tent over here, so you have the bar with some tables out here for people who want to enjoy the scenery. I think it will look wonderful, Karen."

"Wyatt and Jenny are okay with all of this?" Karen asked cautiously.

"We've already been over all this." Kristin put her hands on her hips and sauntered back towards Karen. "I asked them about it, and they said they were happy to do it. They have space and are already working on getting the barn looking its best for your day. Stop worrying about it, Karen. It will be beautiful."

Karen walked back into the barn and stood in the center space, looking up at the ceiling and marveling at the beauty of it all. "Do you think we can leave some of the hay on the floor, and maybe some bales for people to sit around if they want?"

"You bet!" Kristin exclaimed. "Trust me, you will love it even more once it's decorated. There is also room outside down by the lake if you want to have the ceremony there. We can set up the chairs and an archway for you, maybe even get some of the kids from the high school orchestra to come and play music for the ceremony. Oh, and there is an old carriage down at the stables, you can use to ride to the ceremony with a couple of the horses."

Karen looked at Kristin as she went on about all that they could do.

"Sounds like you have thought about this before," Karen said, putting her arm around Kristin.

"Sure, I have," Kristin replied quietly. "Even though Wes and I never talked about it, I imagined getting married here. It's an idyllic spot and has lovely memories for me here."

"That can all still happen, you know," Karen told her.

Kristin shook her head to clear out the images.

"I can't think about any of that right now. We need to concentrate on your day."

"Well, I'm convinced," Karen said, beaming.

"Okay, I'll let Wyatt know, and you start calling everyone involved to make sure they get here for the 22nd. It's only a few weeks left to the date, so we need to move. Oh, Karen, it's going to be a lovely night," Kristin told her.

"Thanks, Kris… for doing this I mean," Karen said, taking her best friend's hand as they walked back towards the car. "I know you're going through a rough patch right now and doing all this here can't be easy for you."

"It was easy for me, Karen. You're my closest friend, and I love Wyatt and Jenny and this place, despite the problems I might be having with Wes right now."

"Let me call Brian and let him know! This is amazing!" Karen answered as she pulled out her cell phone to call her fiancé.

Kristin took another look around the area and envisioned the wedding spot filled with happy faces, the décor, the music, and with her and Wes as the bride and groom. A lump formed in her throat and she looked away quickly to get the vision out of her head.

****

The nine-hour bus ride from Washington to O'Fallon, Missouri, where the Wild Things would play the River City Rascals, was just as Wes thought it would be – long, crowded, and uncomfortable. The team had a beautiful bus with comfortable seating for everyone, which was a far cry from Wes remembered from his days in the minor leagues when he bussed to locations near and far. After having spent the last sixteen years of his life on planes and chartered flights with gourmet meals, this scenario served as an awakening.

The team did stop for lunch along the way at a fast food place to get meals for all twenty-five players, the manager and coach, the equipment staff, and Sabrina, who traveled with the team when on the road and doubled as the traveling secretary as part of her duties.

Wes knew that most of the guys on the team had limited funds to work with, and the daily allotment from the organization made extra pocket money if they made it last. Wes made sure to get to the fast-food counter first to let the cashier know that he wanted to pay for the entire team's order.

Many of the players who were skeptical of Wes on the team appreciated his willingness to do that, and Wes' secretly hoped it might bring him closer to his new teammates so they might be willing to give him a chance. Of course, once the guys heard they didn't need to pay for the meal themselves, many went from ordering off the dollar menu to meals that offered more. The total bill came to almost $400 for Wes, but he was happy to pay it.

Wes had his meal and found an empty table to sit at so he could munch on the chicken sandwich he ordered. When Emil walked past with his tray, he immediately sat down with Wes while some of the other teammates looked on.

"Nice of you to pick up the tab, Wes," Emil said as he ate some French fries. "Getting two meals out of you in the last few days is a real treat. I need to remember to keep hanging out with you."

"Don't get too used to it, Emil," Wes laughed. "Besides, once you are in the big leagues, you will want to remember this. There are going to be younger guys that may need an extra hand now and then."

"Man, I wish I had as much confidence in making it as you do," Emil replied as he squeezed out a ketchup packet onto his burger wrapper to dip fries into. "I'm just grateful to be here."

"I hear you, Emil," Wes answered. "I'm grateful to be here too. But I'm nearing the end of the line. You're just getting started. I've seen you at practice. You've got that special something; keep working at it. Scouts and teams want to see you're hungry and willing to work for it."

John Clines came along to rush the guys through lunch so they could get back on the bus and finish the ride to Missouri. Wes went to dump his garbage into the trash bin and bumped into Sabrina, who stretched to do the same.

"I'm sorry," Wes said. He gallantly stepped aside so Sabrina could go first.

"My, what a gentleman," Sabrina replied. "Thanks for lunch," Sabrina said to Wes.

"My pleasure," he nodded and then held the door open for Sabrina to walk out. Sabrina wore noticeably tight blue jeans and a checkered blouse tied at the waist, hardly an outfit that one might think a representative of the team would wear on the road. Sabrina definitely received notice from all the young men on the bus every step of the way.

The team arrived at their motel by three, which gave them just enough time to unload their things before heading over to the ballpark to prepare for the night game. John Clines divided up the rooms, so everyone got a roommate, allowing the team to save some money. Emil volunteered to room with Wes.

Sabrina approached Wes as they waited outside for their room assignments.

"Do you have a roommate for our stay?" Sabrina asked.

"I guess I will," Wes replied. Just then, Emil walked over, holding a room key, and dangled it in front of Wes.

"We're bunking together," Emil told Wes, handing Wes a key. "Room 225."

Wes gripped the key in his hand as Sabrina looked on.

"Aww, well that's too bad," Sabrina said, pouting. "I'm in 117. See you guys back on the bus in a bit."

Emil and Wes both watched Sabrina walk away as she pulled her wheeled suitcase behind her.

"Damn," Emil whispered. He looked at Wes as they walked towards the staircase to get to their room.

"Are you planning on trying to get with her? I can go bunk with one of the other guys if you want time," Emil offered.

"I… I have someone back at home, Emil, so no, I'm not planning anything."

"Does Sabrina know that?" Emil asked as Wes opened the door to their room.

"I don't have a clue." Wes tried not to think about it at all.

"Well, Wes, she's on the prowl for you, man."

"Just drop your stuff in, Emil, so we can get back on the bus," Wes said to him Wes dropped his duffel bag on one of the beds.

The team hurried back to the bus to get to the stadium but rushing to get there didn't help much. The Rascals outclassed the Wild Things 7-2. The only time Wes moved off the bench during the game was to try and cheer on his teammates, and when Emil got the team on the scoreboard with a two-run home run in the fifth inning. Emil flew around the bases and got back to the dugout greeted by high fives, and he smiled widely at Wes.

"That was all you, man," Emil said as he grabbed a handful of sunflower seeds and sat next to Wes on the bench. "Those tips for my swing really paid off."

"Don't get home run happy just yet, Emil," Wes warned. "You're an excellent line-drive guy. Go for the gaps instead of swinging for the fences all the time. You still have time to grow and fill out your body, and then the home runs will come."

The next few games against River City didn't play out much better. The Wild Things lost all four games, which included shutouts in the last two, leaving a bad taste in the mouth of the manager and the players. It made the five-hour bus trip north from O'Fallon to Schaumberg, Illinois seem even longer than it should be. The team arrived at the hotel at 2 AM, and everyone felt grateful to crawl into bed for the night.

Schaumberg proved miserable as well, with the team losing the first two games of that series. The Wild Things scratched out just one run, again thanks to Emil, who singled, stole second and third, and then scored on a wild pitch. Wes hadn't sniffed a baseball bat or glove for any of the first six games, making him feel like he didn't even need to get his uniform cleaned since it still looked brand new.

After the second game, and after getting chewed out by John Clines for their play, the team went back to the hotel dejected. It was still early in the evening, and once again Wes sent Kristin a few text messages, as he did each day, but he either got no reply or just a sentence that she was okay. Wes stuffed his phone in his jeans pocket and arose from the bed he sat on. Emil and Felix Machado, the team's second baseman, were busy playing basketball on the game console that Felix's parents gave him before the team left for the road trip.

"Where you are going man?" Emil said as he peered around Wes to see the screen as Wes walked by.

"I'm going over to that bar across the street for a drink," Wes answered. "You guys are welcome to join me."

"No can do," Emil said as his video player slam-dunked the basketball, causing Felix to cringe and curse in Dominican. "I'm still underage, and Felix is too."

"Okay, well you kids have a good time and don't stay up too late," Wes said in a parental tone.

Wes shuffled across the parking lot, wearing his leather jacket over his t-shirt and jeans. He arrived at the bar, called The Gypsy, and strode in. It was a local place and only had a few patrons in it, all who were clearly regulars. Wes sat down on the barstool and ordered a beer, figuring this was the kind of place where beer was pretty much all the bartender ever did.

He sipped his beverage and took a quick look up at the TV to see the sports highlights of the Cubs and Pirates going on. Wes thought about the times he visited Chicago with the team, how he loved playing at Wrigley on days when the wind blew out, and how he would always go out to the ivy-covered walls before the game to run his hands through the leaves and think about all the players who played on the same field many years before him.

Wes drank about half of his beer when he spun around on his barstool to survey the rest of the place. He noticed the obligatory pool table and dartboard towards the back of the establishment, and a few booths along the far wall that had dim, dingy lighting over them. A hand casually raised and waved in Wes' direction from one of the booths, and upon a closer look, Wes saw Sabrina, by herself, sipping a cocktail.

Wes knew it was unavoidable, and he would have to go over and say hello. He sauntered over and sat on the opposite side of the booth from Sabrina.

"Nice to see a friendly face here," Sabrina said as she sipped her drink.

Wes just smiled and nodded, unsure of what to say.

"I'm glad you're here," Sabrina said, leaning over the table towards Wes so that she flashed a clear view down her cleavage as she spoke. "You can protect me from anyone that comes over to try to pick me up."

"Something tells me you're pretty good at taking care of yourself," Wes replied as he sat back and drank his beer.

"Hmmm, you are an observant man, aren't you? I like a man that sees everything and has experience."

The burly bartender wandered over and cleared empty glasses off the table from the booth behind Wes and Sabrina.

"Get you two another?" he rasped.

"Sure," Wes said, as he saw Sabrina's drink was empty. "I'll have another beer." He looked at Sabrina, who smiled at the bartender and handed her empty glass to him.

"I'll have another bourbon on the rocks," Sabrina told him.

The bartender went off to do his job, and Wes looked back at Sabrina, who had spread her arms out on the top of the booth like a falcon spreads its wings before swooping in for a prey. She pushed her chest out a bit more as she sat and stared at Wes hungrily.

"Bourbon," Wes said casually. "Nice choice."

"I love it," Sabrina answered. "A bourbon that fills my mouth and tastes smooth when it first enters and then gives me that slow burn as it glides down my throat… it's delectable."

Wes felt much warmer now in his leather jacket and fidgeted in the booth.

"So, Wes," Sabrina began, "tell me a bit more about yourself. Something I can't learn from the Internet or Wikipedia. I know where you're from and about your playing days, and I know you have a daughter, but I haven't seen a wedding ring on your hand."

Wes fidgeted some more as he became noticeably uncomfortable with the conversation.

"I'm not married," Wes said politely. "My wife and I divorced years ago. I do have someone back home in Chandler," Wes told her, "at least I think I do."

The bartender arrived with fresh drinks, and Wes immediately picked up his beer and started to indulge.

"You think you do," Sabrina said boldly. "Things not all hunky-dory at home? That happens a lot with ballplayers. It's hard to have a relationship when you're away a lot. I guess that's why a lot of players don't do it. They just enjoy the bachelor life and have fun when they can."

"Well, Kristin and I have been together for over a year now, but this is the first time we've really been apart. It's a difficult situation; I don't really want to get into it," Wes said.

"Kristin," Sabrina said as she sipped her bourbon, tinkling the ice in her glass after her drink.

"Lovely name. Well, I'm sure it will all work out for the best for you, whatever you do."

Sabrina sat back again, and Wes noticed it looked as though she undid another button on the black satin blouse she wore, baring even more of her breasts.

It was then that John Clines appeared next to the booth, and disappointment shot across Sabrina's face.

"Didn't expect to find anyone from the team here," John said as he slid into the booth next to Sabrina.

"Please, join us, John," Sabrina said sarcastically.

"Most of the guys are too young to drink, and the others would be breaking curfew if they were here," John said as he glared at Wes.

"You can fine me if you want, John, or sit me out tomorrow for being out past curfew. It's not like I have to worry about getting to bed in time to play." Wes took a long draw of his beer, nearly draining the mug.

"That's where you're wrong. Martin," John said as he took a drink of his own beer. "You're in tomorrow at DH. I'm going to bat you fifth."

Wes' eyes went wide with surprise. "Really? What changed your mind?"

"Three things," John answered. "First, we stink right now and haven't scored a run in three games. Second, I've noticed what you've done with Emil, taking him under your wing, helping him out, and it's paid off for him. He's the only guy in the lineup doing anything right now, so maybe you can rub off on some of the other guys."

"And what's the third thing?" Wes asked.

"Well, third is I'm tired of Tom calling me after every game asking me why I haven't used you in the lineup. Hopefully, this will get him off my back for a bit. Either you get some hits, or you play awful; either way, it helps me."

"Gee, thanks John," Wes said as he finished his beer and got out of the booth. "I guess I better get back to the hotel and get some rest then. Have a good night, you two."

Sabrina stretched out her arm, trying to get Wes' attention before he departed, but John turned to her and talked, and she slumped back into the booth, trapped.

When Wes returned to the hotel, Emil lounged on his bed, going over messages on his phone.

"Game over?" Wes asked, noticing Felix was gone.

"Yeah, I was kicking Felix's ass so bad he started to rage in Dominican, and I couldn't understand what he was yelling at me about. I'm pretty sure it was mostly swear words. He took his stuff and went back to his room. What are you doing back already?"

"I need to get some rest," Wes said. "John told me I'm playing tomorrow." Wes tossed his jeans on the chair by his bed and got under the blanket.

"Hey, Wes, that's great!" Emil said. "Oh, I have to answer this text from my Mom. She checks up on me every night at this time."

Wes plugged in his phone and looked to see if there were any messages for him. All he saw was a brief note from Izzy, saying goodnight and that she hoped he had a good day. He picked up his phone and messaged her back:

Not bad. Could be better, but I'm actually playing tomorrow. Talk to you after the game. We head back to Washington. I hope the play is going well. Miss you and love you.

Wes sent the message, then thought about posting a similar one to Kristin, but instead, put his phone down and shut the light off.

18

Kristin spent more nights at Wes' house the last few days because it gave her a chance to both work on the wedding plans going on at the barn and spend some time with Izzy, something she hadn't done enough of lately in Kristin's mind. Kristin would either pick Izzy up after rehearsals or meet her at home after work so that they cooked dinner together and talked. Kristin enjoyed every minute of it and got to laugh and relax with Izzy so that she didn't overthink being in Wes' home without him.

It was a warmer evening, nice enough where they opened the back door to the patio to let the breeze wash through the house and provide some clean, spring air. Kristin came home with Izzy after rehearsals, and the two decided to make a simple stir fry dinner of chicken and broccoli.

"How's the musical going?" Kristin asked as she chopped the broccoli. "You only have four days until opening night."

"I know," Izzy said as she placed the white rice in the rice cooker and set it. "I'm starting to feel a little nervous about it. I'm going to be in front of all those people acting and singing. It's kind of scary."

"You'll do fine," Kristin reassured her. "You know, maybe… maybe you should call your Dad and tell him about it. He has gotten in front of thousands of people each night. I'm sure there are days where he gets the jitters. He might be able to help you."

"Yeah, I can do that," Izzy added. "I know he has a game tonight," Izzy looked at the clock to see it was nearly seven. "I'll have to wait until it is over. You know he told me he was playing tonight."

"Is that right," Kristin said, not looking up from the onion she was slicing.

"It's not on TV since it's independent ball, but I think it's on the radio online. We… we can listen if you want," Izzy said hesitantly.

"Izzy, we can definitely do that," Kristin told her as she placed the vegetables in the hot wok and steam billowed up right away. "Just because your Dad and I are… having issues… doesn't mean we can't support him. I don't hate him or anything. I care about him very deeply, you know that."

"Have… have you talked to him?" Izzy asked, passing Kristin a glass bowl to put the vegetables in.

"No, no, I haven't," Kristin admitted. "We've texted a couple of times, but that's it."

"He's struggled, Kris," Izzy told her. "He hasn't played, and I know he's feeling homesick… and he really misses you. They'll be back in Washington tomorrow for their home opener."

Kristin tossed the chicken pieces into the wok and heard them sizzle as they hit the oil.

"Did you want to go to the game?" Kristin asked her.

"I do, but I can't, we have dress rehearsals, and I have to be there. Grandma and Grandpa can't go either. Grandma has an appointment with her oncologist, and they can't miss it. Someone should be there to support Dad."

"Izzy," Kristin said as she stirred the chicken and then put the broccoli and vegetables back in before she poured the tangy sauce Izzy made over the food. "I don't know if I can."

"Come on, Kris," Izzy begged. "He really needs someone right now."

"Okay," Kristin said resignedly. "I will go. It will be fun. I've never been to a live baseball game before."

"You'll love it, and Dad will be so happy. I'll text him to let him know," Izzy said as she picked up her phone.

"No, Izzy," Kristin said, as she placed her hand over Izzy's phone. "Please don't let him know. I'm not sure how I would be if I talked to him in-person just yet. Let's keep it a surprise for now."

"Okay," Izzy said.

Izzy put her phone down and then picked up each dinner plate and scooped some rice onto each. Kristin poured the chicken and broccoli into a serving bowl, and the two went to sit at the kitchen table to eat.

After a few forkfuls of food, Izzy looked up at Kristin.

"I didn't tell you about Bradley," Izzy said, rolling her eyes.

"Why, what's wrong?" Kristin asked as she stabbed a piece of chicken with her fork.

"He's all bent out of shape about the musical because there are a couple of scenes where I have to kiss Justin. I mean, he is the prince after all! Ariel is supposed to kiss the prince! I tried to explain to him that it's just acting, but he doesn't want to hear it."

"Well, I guess it's natural for him to feel a little jealous when someone else is kissing his girl. Once the play is over, it will all be fine," Kristin told her.

"I hope so because he's making me nuts," Izzy said. "Boys can be so confusing."

"You said it, sister," Kristin replied, raising her glass of iced tea to Izzy.

****

Wes' first performance with the Wild Things the night before disappointed him. He batted four times, striking out three of them and getting a single in his last at-bat to break the ice. Unfortunately, the team got creamed 9-1, and the long trip back to Washington seemed like it might never end. Wes prayed that the next game would be better.

The following day, Wes put his uniform on, as usual, and headed out to the field for pregame warmups. He stretched and exercised, took a brief jog in the outfield, and even took some fielding practice at first base, although there were no plans for him to be in the field tonight. Wes always wanted to be prepared just in case. He also took his regular batting practice, though he was allowed more swings tonight because he was in the lineup.

The combination of it being Opening Day, and Tom promoting the fact that Wes was going to be in the lineup, ensured that the stadium would be at capacity. The stadium only held about 3,200 people, but by the time the grounds crew groomed the field and painted the lines, the place looked filled and buzzed with anticipation.

As excited as Wes was to be in the lineup, he was also a bit disappointed because he knew he wouldn't have anyone in the stands rooting for him. Izzy told him she had dress rehearsals, and his parents had a specialist appointment that his mother could not miss. Wes texted Kristin, as he always did, but this time to let her know he would leave a ticket for her if she wanted to come. He never heard back from her, so he wasn't expecting her to show up.

The game against the Lake Erie Crushers would be a tough one. Lake Erie had a good team and had scored a lot runs already in the young season, which didn't bode well for the Wild Things, whose pitching struggled to start the season. No matter the outcome, Wes was just happy to get a chance to show what he could do in front of a home crowd.

The Wild Things took the field to thunderous applause from the crowd. Each player on the team got introduced separately and tipped their hat, and it was apparent what host families had each player by the smatterings of extra applause received when they were announced. It then came time to announce the starting lineups. Emil was announced as the leadoff hitter, and the crowd gave him a good ovation, knowing he was the one player doing well so far. When it came to the fifth slot, and they announced Wes, he jogged out onto the field and was shocked that he received a standing ovation from the fans. Wes smiled and waved his hat genially as he soaked in the appreciation before stepping back into line.

As the rest of lineup got announced, Wes scanned the crowd behind home plate to see if Kristin appeared. He knew what seat they had given her since the field level seats were actual seats, unlike the bench seating that occupied most of the stadium. He saw that her seat remained empty, and his heart sunk a bit.

While the Wild Things were pumped up for the start of the game, and the fans were into it, the Lake Erie Crushers silenced everyone in the top of the first. The first two batters each doubled, and then a hit batter, a walk, and a grand slam made it 5-0 before the Wild Things even got off the field. The crowd grew despondent despite the antics and games that went before the bottom half of the inning started.

    Emil got the game started right for the team by singling to center and stealing second, and Felix, batting second, bunted for a base hit, but the next two batters struck out. That brought Wes up to the plate. He stepped into the box to face a live pitcher in a home game for the first time in over a year and suddenly felt eighteen again and a kid just starting out. The pitcher in front of him wasn't more than twenty-one or twenty-two and looked a little in awe of Wes standing there taking his practice swings. The Crushers manager shouted out to his pitcher, "Come on, Langford, you got this! This guy's too old to do anything."

    Wes glared over at the opposing dugout and spotted the manager of the Crushers, and recognized him immediately - Wendell Roth. Wendell was a minor league player Wes saw in Pirates camp for a few years that never made it beyond AA ball and now managed instead. He gave Wendell a nod and dug in at the plate.

    The first two pitches to Wes were high and away fastballs. Wes glanced at the scoreboard, thinking he might see how fast the pitcher threw, but the scoreboard didn't record those stats. Wes figured he was in the low 90s, which was good, but not unhittable. It made him wonder if the pitcher had a change of pace or curveball to throw at all.

    Wes found out quickly when Langford laid a change-up in that sat right in the middle of the plate. Wes took a smooth swing and saw the ball jump off his bat and loft high and deep to right field, quickly clearing the fence just to the right of the scoreboard.

The stadium erupted with cheers as Wes made his way around the bases, and Emil and Felix greeted him happily at home plate. Wes took a quick glance over and saw Kristin's seat still empty.

The dugout was elated at the turn of events, and it sparked a rally, so the Wild Things scored one more run, making it 5-4 after the first inning. The teams went back and forth, with neither pitching well. When Wes came up again in the third, Langford, who struggled, wanted no part of him and kept everything in the dirt so that Wes walked. The same happened when Wes came up in the fifth, and again in the seventh, and the crowd booed each time he got a free pass to first.

By the time the ninth inning rolled around, the crowd had grown anxious and on edge. The score was 8-7 Crushers, and they had just brought in their best reliever, Steve Matthews. Emil led off the inning with a single and Felix bunted him over to second. Unfortunately, the next batter struck out and then their cleanup hitter, Forrest Duncan, hit a weak foul pop up caught by the third baseman. Once again, it was left to Wes.

Wes knew they wouldn't walk him now. He represented the winning run, and the Crushers wouldn't take the chance of putting him on base. Matthews pitched to him, and threw two wicked fastballs, one on the outside corner and then one under Wes' chin, causing him to bend out of the way. Wes saw Matthews' cockiness and figured Matthews would throw another fastball.

Wes was right, and the ball was on the outside corner again. This time, Wes reached it, sending it screaming down the left line, not where the Crushers had the outfield shifted. The ball took one hop and hit the fence, dying there, but the left fielder was shaded so far over towards centerfield that he had to race towards the ball to get it. Emil jogged home from second base and Wes, knowing he had to find another gear to make it, ran harder than he had in a long time. He slid feet first into third, ahead of the relay throw, and popped up on the base safely.

The soreness appeared back in Wes' ankle the moment he got to the base. He hadn't tested it well since bruising it all those months ago and sliding on it may have aggravated it slightly. He reached down to rub it while the Crushers manager went for a mound visit to talk with his pitcher.

John Clines, who coached third along with managing, came over to Wes.

"Nice hitting," he said, patting Wes on the back. "You okay? That was a lot of running and a rough slide. I can put a pinch-runner in if you need it."

"I'm okay," Wes huffed, resting his hands on his knees.

As the Crushers met on the mound, Wes glanced behind home plate. There, with her blond hair tucked under a Wild Things hat, sat Kristin. She caught Wes' eye and gave him a thumbs-up sign as she smiled. Wes smiled back, standing up straight. He suddenly felt reinvigorated and ready to go.

The Crushers moved the infield and outfield in, hoping to cut down the potential winning run. Wes took a small lead with their third baseman, Bobby Marsh, standing in the box. It was then Wes got an idea. He took a bit of a more significant lead, going down to meet where the Crushers' third baseman was stationed. Wes knew he could lead as far down as the third baseman was positioned and still get back to third in time if he had to, but he also figured that leading that far down the line would rattle Matthews.

Matthews looked over at Wes again and again, and Wes bluffed running down the line, so much so that Matthews stepped off the rubber to compose himself. Wendell Roth yelled to his pitcher.

"Matthews! He's an out of breath old man! He's not going anywhere. Concentrate on the batter!"

Wes smiled and then retook his big lead, bluffing once more, and this time winked at Matthews as he did. Matthews was stunned, so much so that he flinched on the mound while still on the rubber.

"Balk!" the home plate umpire yelled and waved Wes home.

Wes trotted down the line and stepped on home plate, scoring the winning run as the crowd went wild. Wendell Roth sprang out of the Crusher's dugout, red-faced and screaming at the umpire about the call, but it was correct. Wes' teammates all came out and jumped around him as Wes laughed. He caught a glimpse of Kristin clapping and smiling in the crowd as he headed into the dugout.

The team celebrated its first win in the locker room while a fireworks display went on in the stadium to entertain the crowd. Tom Killian rushed into the locker room with a couple of photographers to get pictures of Wes for the team's website and social media, and for the local newspaper. Wes did his best to get through all the questions and everything else as quickly and as politely as he could because he wanted to get out to see Kristin. Once the last interview ended, he dressed as fast as he could and left the locker room.

Wes halted just outside the locker room. Emil and Felix both stood there in their street clothes.

"Wes, come on out with us. We're going to celebrate! I mean, as much as we can celebrate at Chili's anyway," Emil told him.

Wes gazed passed Emil and saw Kristin standing there, about twenty feet away. She was wearing the yellow dress that Wes had bought for her last spring because he loved the way it looked on her.

"Sorry boys," Wes said, as he parted the way through Emil and Felix and went over to where Kristin was.

"You came," Wes said softly. "I didn't think you were going to be here. I left the ticket for you but your seat…"

Kristin interrupted.

"I know, I'm sorry I was a bit late getting here, and then they couldn't find the ticket for me, it was a big mess. I'm sorry I missed your home run."

"I don't even care about that," Wes answered.

Wes took Kristin's hand, and they started to walk away together. Suddenly, Emil, who had dashed over, cut them off.

"Wes, aren't you at least going to introduce me to your pretty lady friend?" Emil said with a smile.

"Kristin Arthur, this is Emil Stanton," Wes said as he rolled his eyes.

"Pleasure to meet you, Emil," Kristin said politely, offering her hand.

Emil gave her hand a light handshake.

"Your boyfriend here is a standup guy. He's been a big help to me, looking out for me and everything. I can't say enough good things about him."

"That's great, Emil," Kristin replied. "I saw you play tonight. You were terrific."

"Well, thank you, Kristin. Hey, this young lady is beautiful, kind, and sweet. How did an old grump like you land her?" Emil asked. "Kristin, you don't happen to have a sister, do you? I could use someone like you in my life."

"I do have a sister, Emil, but she lives in Georgia. Sorry."

"Well that is a shame," Emil said, shaking his head.

"Okay, enough of this," Wes interrupted. He spun Emil around and pointed him towards Felix. "Felix is waiting for you. Go to Chili's and have a good time. Here." Wes reached into his wallet and pulled out fifty dollars. "Dinner is on me, go."

"See, Kristin," Emil said with a smile, holding the fifty, "the man is always looking out for me. Nice to meet you."

Wes pushed Emil in the direction of Felix and then grabbed Kristin's hand and ran towards his truck.

"He seems nice," Kristin giggled.

"Yeah, he's a beaut alright," Wes said as he opened the car door for Kristin. Before she could climb in, Wes took hold of Kristin and kissed her deeply. Kristin gasped lightly at first but then melted into his arms and kissed him back.

"I've wanted to do that since the moment I saw you here. Even before I saw you here. For the last month," Wes said, bending down to kiss her again. "Let's go."

He guided Kristin into the passenger seat and ran over to the driver's side to get in. Wes drove with a mission, back to the Ramada and pulled into a parking spot, squealing the tires and brakes as he got there.

Wes jumped out of the truck and opened the door for Kristin to get out. Once she was out, he took her by the hand and led her directly inside and over to the elevator. The doors slid open quickly, and the two jumped inside. Wes pressed the Door Close button several times to shut the doors before anyone else got on the elevator. As the elevator moved, Wes pulled Kristin to him once more so they could kiss again. Wes' hands roamed all over Kristin's body. He placed his hands on her waist and pushed her against the back wall of the elevator, slipping his tongue gently into her mouth as they kissed more.

Wes moved his hands up from Kristin's waist to the yellow buttons that went down the front of her dress. One by one, he started to undo the buttons until he had undone them all down to her waist.

"Wes," Kristin gasped, "what if someone else comes in the elevator?"

"I'm up on the fifth floor. We're almost there," Wes said as he looked at the floor indicator before turning back to touching Kristin. His hands slipped inside the open part of her dress, cupping her breasts encased in her yellow bra. Kristin became caught up in the moment as well, reaching her right hand down to feel Wes bulging through his jeans.

Naturally, the elevator came to a stop on the fourth floor. Kristin noticed the doors sliding open and pushed Wes back a bit so that she could pull the top of her dress together. An older couple stood and stared for a moment as Wes and Kristin stared back.

The gentleman had his mouth open, while the woman took his hand.

"We're looking for the down elevator, Vincent," she said to her companion. "This one is clearly going up," she said, giving a sly grin to Kristin and Wes.

The doors slid closed, and Wes and Kristin both broke out in raucous laughter.

When the elevator finally reached the fifth floor, Wes peeked out to make sure no one was in the hallway. The two then made a mad dash to Wes' room, Kristin fighting to keep her bra covered as she ran. Once Wes got the door open, he dragged Kristin inside and then placed the 'Do Not Disturb' sign on the door.

"I'm not taking any chances," Wes said as he closed and locked the door.

Wes stripped out of his t-shirt and kicked his sneakers off before he even reached Kristin on the bed. Kristin let her dress fall open before pushing it down her body, leaving her in just her yellow bra and panties. Wes took his cue and removed his jeans, not wanting to waste a second more. He then leaped on the bed, causing Kristin to bounce up a bit and shriek loudly.

"Wes!" she yelled before coming to rest in his arms.

"I have missed you so much," Wes whispered before he began kissing Kristin's neck.

Kristin brought her hands up to Wes' head, cradling it, and pulled him from her neck so she could look at him.

"Wes, you have to know that it was difficult for me to be apart from you. I just felt like we needed this time to see what we each really wanted."

"Kris, I've known all along what I wanted. I just got a little distracted along the way, and I'm sorry about that. The way that things are… I don't want to be apart from you, and if that means I have to give up baseball…"

"I never said you should, Wes," Kristin insisted. "I just wanted to know that I was a long-term part of your life and involved in what we decide is best for us as a couple. Let's not…"

Wes kissed Kristin hungrily and cut her off and moved above Kristin.

"We can talk about it later," Wes told her, moving down to kiss her breasts through her bra.

Wes deftly reached behind Kristin and unhooked the bra, and Kristin shook it off and tossed it away so that Wes could continue. As he cupped her breasts, his tongue worked slowly around each nipple, lightly flicking across the tip to send bolts of ecstasy through Kristin's body. Each touch, kiss, and nibble made Kristin arch her back to get herself closer to Wes, allowing the warmth building inside her to touch against the arousal building in his briefs.

Wes continued teasing Kristin's breasts with his tongue while his left hand moved down across her taut belly and came to rest on the front of her moist panties. Just the slightest touch outside, combined with what he was doing to her breasts, made Kristin's whole body tingle and want to explode. He touched, licked and teased her all over until Kristin couldn't take it anymore.

"Wes… I need you… I need to feel you…" she implored.

Kristin's hands moved to push Wes' briefs down, freeing him. Her right hand immediately ran to grab his thick erection, and she could feel its strength and desire with that first touch. She began to slowly stroke him as Wes tried to keep up with his teasing of his own. It was a clash of wills as Wes placed his palm over Kristin's mound through her panties, making her moan in pleasure. Kristin followed that with a move of her own, gliding her palm over the head of his penis, taunting it with light pressure.

Wes pulled his face away from her breasts and gasped on his own.

"No fair," Wes growled.

"All's fair in love…" Kristin started to say before Wes slipped a finger into her panties and inside to feel how wet Kristin had become. She moaned loudly this time, pushing her hips up so she could meet Wes' fingers. Her own hand moved from Wes to grip the sides of the pillow her head was on as she writhed in pleasure.

Finally, Wes gently eased Kristin's panties down her legs so she could kick them off. He positioned himself over her again, and slowly, achingly slowly, moved into her. Both shuddered and groaned and that feeling, knowing it had been far too long since they had experienced this pleasure together. Wes slowly built a rhythm, rocked back and forth, as their hips moved in unison. Kristin pulled Wes down to her, kissing him deeply, holding him tightly to her as they moved. Kristin could take no more, and she arched and groaned into Wes' mouth as they kissed, feeling wave after wave of pleasure wash over her.

The way Kristin's body tightened around Wes was all he needed to get pushed over the edge himself. He thrust deeply into her and came, keeping his body pressed against hers so they could repeatedly kiss as their pleasure together subsided.

"Oh, God, that was…" Wes was at a loss for words.

"Amazing? Because it was," Kristin noted. "I guess that's what they mean about make-up sex," she laughed.

Kristin put her head on Wes' shoulder as he held her in his arms, kissing her sweetly over and over. After lying in bed together for a while, Kristin turned to Wes, who had closed his eyes and had a grin on his face.

"Wes?" she said softly.

"Hmmm," he responded, keeping his eyes closed.

"I'm famished."

Wes opened his eyes and rolled over to face Kristin.

"What do you want? I can get room service, anything you like," he told her, sitting up and grabbing the phone.

"Well, I'm careful about what I eat and drink," Kristin remarked. "I've still had issues and figured that maybe I wasn't eating right."

"Did you go to the doctor?" Wes asked with concern.

"Oh yeah," Kristin answered quickly. "She gave me some pills to take, and they have helped, but she still thinks I need to watch what I eat."

"Okay, then you tell me what you want. If the hotel doesn't have it here, I can go out and get it."

"No, I don't want you to do that," Kristin said as she sat up next to him.

"Kris, it's no big deal. There's a convenience store down the street, a Chinese food place, pizza, burgers, you name it. You tell me."

Kristin stared at Wes before answering.

"I really feel like having a small cup of soft-serve vanilla ice cream," she said with a smile.

"That's all you want? You said you were famished."

"I may have exaggerated a little. Sometimes a little bit of ice cream is all a girl needs. Forget about it," Kristin said, pulling the bed sheet up over her breasts.

"No Ma'am," Wes said, jumping out of bed. He grabbed his briefs and jeans off the floor and put them on. "My lady wants soft-serve, that's what she will get. I think there's a Dairy Queen somewhere around here. I'll find it and be back in a few minutes."

Wes slipped his sneakers on, sans socks, and went to grab his t-shirt, but Kristin scooped it up instead.

"Uh-uh, I'm putting this on," she said as she sexily slipped the t-shirt over her head. "And nothing else."

Wes hurried to his drawer and grabbed another t-shirt, then the keys to his truck, and gave Kristin a quick kiss.

"Hold that thought," he said. "And don't put anything else on."

Kristin laughed as Wes darted out the door.

Wes had been gone for about fifteen minutes, and Kristin bathed in the afterglow of their experience together. She lifted the collar of his t-shirt, inhaling so she could take in the manly smell that she loved so much about him. Kristin resolved that they were back on track and that their future together was going to bring great things.

A knock on the door made Kristin turn and face the door before she moved towards the door to open it.

"Did you forget your key?" She asked. "See, that didn't take long at…"

Kristin opened the door to see a woman standing there, holding a bottle of champagne and two glasses. She was dressed in a maroon blouse that was open two buttons too far and a tight black leather skirt. The two women stared at each other without either one saying anything.

"Can… Can I help you?" Kristin stammered, trying to pull the hem down of the t-shirt that suddenly seemed way too short.

"I was looking for Wes," the other woman said, before smiling at her. "Oh, you must be Kristin. Wes mentioned you in passing."

The woman moved past Kristin and into the room without asking and sat down at the small table in the corner.

"I'm sorry, who are you?" Kristin said, staring and still holding the open door.

"I'm Sabrina," she said with a smile, crossing her legs and letting her black leather heel dangle from her left foot. "I guess Wes didn't tell you about me. I can't say I'm surprised."

Kristin let go of the door, and it slammed shut.

"What are you talking about? I'm Wes' girlfriend," Kristin said with emphasis.

"Oh, I know who you are," Sabrina said confidently. "Wes told me that you two had a bit of a falling out recently. I was just stopping by to you know, celebrate his big game. I think you know what I mean," Sabrina gave Kristin a Cheshire Cat grin.

"What? But Wes… we just…" Kristin was at a loss for words.

"He probably just wanted one more tumble for old time's sake. You know how these athletes are. You were just the first game of the doubleheader, honey."

****

Wes returned to the room, juggling what he had purchased at Dairy Queen as he slid the key card into the door.

"Kris, I got your ice cream, and some extra whipped cream and chocolate sauce, in case, well, in case you wanted to try some," he laughed. The room was empty, but the bathroom door was closed with the water running.

Wes put everything down on the table and spotted the champagne and glasses there.

"Hey, where did the champagne come from?" Wes asked.

"I brought it," a voice said, and Wes' head snapped up. There stood Sabrina, dressed in the black t-shirt that Kristin wore when he had left.

"Sabrina, what the hell are you doing here? Where's Kristin?" Wes barked.

"Oh, Kristin, she's charming Wes, she really is. The epitome of a small-town girl. But that's all she is, Wes – just a girl. You need a woman in your life, someone strong, take charge, someone who can keep up with you."

"Sabrina, what the fuck did you do?"

"I just laid out the facts for her is all, Wes," Sabrina said as she started to open the champagne. "I told her you said that you were having trouble, and I thought you needed someone that was more your speed."

Sabrina approached Wes with a glass of champagne, trying to hand one to him. Wes slapped it out of her hand, shattering the glass against the wall.

"Ooh, don't worry, Wes. I like it rough," Sabrina said, pushing herself against his body.

"Get out!" Wes yelled.

Sabrina took two steps back and stared at Wes.

"Are you fucking serious? You're going to choose that goody-two-shoes nothing over me? You don't know what you're passing up."

Sabrina reached down and started to pull the t-shirt off.

"That's it," Wes said gruffly.

He grabbed Sabrina's hands and led her towards the door, opening it up and pushing her out. Two seconds later, he opened the door again and tossed Sabrina's clothes and belongings out to her as well. Sabrina stood there, stunned.

"You're an asshole, Wes! A has-been asshole!" Sabrina screamed. She gathered everything up in a ball and marched off down the hallway.

Wes sat on his bed and frantically dialed Kristin's cell phone. Unsurprisingly, it went right to voicemail.

"Kris, I don't know where you are or what happened here, but you have to believe me when I say there's nothing between Sabrina and me. I don't know what she said or did, but none of it is true. Please, call me back."

Wes tossed his phone down, trying to figure out where Kristin went and what he should do next to try to fix this mess.

19

Kristin got down to the lobby in tears and blindsided by what happened. Her first thought was that she needed to get away from the hotel before Wes got back. There was no way Kristin could face him again. She didn't have her car with her at the hotel and had Karen drop her off at the stadium since she was coming this way to see Brian anyway. She tried Karen's number twice, but Karen didn't answer either time. After the second voicemail, she left Karen a quick message.

"Karen, please call me as soon as you can," she said through sobs.

Kristin walked up to the front desk, wiping tears from her eyes. The young man at the counter looked stunned to see her this way.

"Is everything alright, Ma'am?" he asked.

"Could… could you please get me a cab, as soon as possible, please?"

"Of course, Ma'am." The desk clerk picked up the phone, pressed a button, and called a cab, telling them it was urgent.

"They have a driver in the area. He'll be pulling up in a minute. Do you need help?" the clerk said with concern.

"No, thank you. You've been very helpful," Kristin said as she walked out the sliding glass doors.

Within a minute, a cab pulled up in front of the hotel and Kristin climbed in.

"Hello," the driver said to her in a friendly tone. "My name is Harry. Where can I take you?"

Kristin gazed out the window and saw Wes walk towards the front of the hotel from the parking lot, carrying the ice cream she asked for.

"Miss?" the driver questioned.

"Can you take me over to the mall?" she said quickly.

"Miss, it's after eleven. The mall closed over an hour ago."

"It's okay, I'm meeting someone there, please, just go," she pleaded.

"Whatever you say," the driver replied.

The cab pulled away with Kristin crouching down so Wes wouldn't see her leaving.

The mall was just moments away, and Kristin asked the driver to pull around to where the restaurant was, knowing they were probably just closing and leaving for the night. She handed the driver twenty dollars for a $2.50 fare and told him to keep the change as she climbed out of the car.

The driver pulled away, and Kristin scanned the parking lot for the cars that remained. She waited just a few minutes before Brian came out of the restaurant door, his jacket slung over his shoulder.

"Brian?" Kristin voiced.

Brian looked up and saw Kristin there, tears drying on her face.

"Kris? What are you doing here? Karen said she dropped you off at the game to be with Wes. Why are you crying? Is everything okay?"

"Brian… can you please… please take me home?" Kristin wept.

"Of course," Brian said, putting his arm around Kristin. "I'll take you to my apartment. Karen is there waiting for me."

The two got into Brian's car, and he started off towards his place. Along the way, he pressed the Bluetooth on his steering wheel and called his apartment number to reach Karen.

"Hey there, Tiger," Karen purred. "I can't wait for you to get here. I'm wearing that leopard thing you like so much and we…"

"Karen!" Brian interrupted, "I… I have Kris in the car with me."

"Kris? What's wrong?" Karen asked.

Kristin started crying again.

"I… I was with Wes… and everything was great… and he went out to get ice cream, and then this other woman showed up, and she said she and Wes were… Karen, it was a mess. I just ran out of there. Can… can you take me home, please?"

"Of course, sweetie," Karen said to her. "I'll meet you guys in the parking lot."

Brian hung up the phone and kept driving silently.

"Thank you so much, Brian," Kristin told him. "I'm sorry I ruined your evening."

"Hey, it's not a problem, really," Brian assured her. "The wedding is in a few days anyway. We should… I mean…" Brian was all flustered.

"It's okay, you don't have to explain… Tiger," Kristin said, wiping her eyes and smiling.

Brian pulled into his parking spot, and Karen was already outside, waiting for them to arrive. She opened the passenger door, and Kristin got out, immediately falling into Karen's arms. Karen held Kristin and hugged her to console her.

"Tell me what happened," Karen asked.

Kristin went into the story of what happened with each detail. When she was done, Kristin felt spent.

"I can't believe Wes would do that," Karen said. "Something's not right about this."

"It all seemed pretty clear to me," Kristin insisted. "I don't know what to think anymore. Oh God, I'm gonna be sick."

Kristin turned back towards Brian's car.

"No, not in the car!" Brian yelled.

It was already too late as Kristin vomited all over the front passenger seat and the dashboard not once, but twice.

"Oh man," Brian bemoaned.

"Brian relax," Karen chided. "We can clean the car… well, I mean you can clean it," Karen said, looking at the mess and taking in the smell.

"Come on, Kris," Karen said to her friend. "Let's go back to my house." Karen guided Kristin over to her car.

"I'll call you when I get home," Karen said to Brian, leaving him to stare into the open door of his car. Brian just nodded his head as he tried to figure out how he was going to clean up.

****

After trying to reach Kristin by phone, Wes raced down the stairwell to the lobby floor and ran to the front desk.

"Excuse me," he panted. "Did you see a woman in a yellow dress, she was probably upset, maybe crying."

"Yes sir, I did," the clerk explained. "I called her a cab about fifteen or twenty minutes ago. It's been a weird night. First her crying and then some woman screaming and cursing all through the lobby wearing nothing but a t-shirt. I almost had to call the police."

"You probably should have," Wes muttered.

"Do you know what cab company you called?"

"Yes, sir, Confident Cab company. Do you need a cab, sir?" the clerk asked.

"No, I just need to talk to the driver that picked her up," Wes said, getting exasperated.

"Oh, that's easy enough. This time of night during the week it's always Harry over here. He's probably out front waiting to see if anyone needs a ride." The clerk pointed to the front door.

"Thanks," Wes said as he walked outside, fixing the sneaker that was untied that kept slipping off.

Wes looked around and saw a cab parked under one of the lights in the parking lot just beyond the hotel entrance. He jogged over to the taxi and knocked on the driver's side window rapidly.

The cabbie tentatively rolled down the window, and a puff of smoke came from the cab. Wes recognized the aroma right away.

"Harry, I need you to answer some questions," Wes demanded.

"Dude, are you a cop? Because I hardly have any weed in here. Not enough for a ticket anyway," Harry told him, his eyes glazed over.

"Harry I'm not a cop..." Wes went on.

"Well I hope you don't need a ride right now, 'cause I'm kind of baked," Harry said, giggling to himself.

"I don't need a ride, I need you to focus, Harry," Wes said while he grabbed Harry's denim jacket collar.

"Okay, okay," Harry insisted.

"You picked up a woman at this hotel a little bit ago. A woman in a yellow dress, remember?"

Harry considered the question. "Oh yeah, a really nice lady. Gave me twenty dollars for a $2.50 fare and said: 'Harry, keep the change.'" Harry laughed again.

"Great Harry," Wes told him. "I'll give you a hundred if you tell me where you took her."

"No way," Harry said, staring at Wes.

Wes opened his wallet and took out a hundred-dollar bill and held it in front of Harry.

"Where did you take her?" Wes insisted.

"Over to the mall," Harry said. "I told her it was closed, but she had me take her around to the restaurant entrance and leave her there."

"Thanks, Harry," Wes said, handing him the bill.

"You bet," Harry yelled as Wes ran off towards his truck. "You need any other information, you come to Harry!"

Wes jumped in his truck and headed out towards Brian's apartment, figuring that is who Kristin looked for. He drove his vehicle quickly over I-70 to where he thought Brian's apartment was but found the wrong place and had to double back until he found the right one. Wes pulled up and saw Brian on his hands and knees at the passenger side of his car.

"Brian!" Wes yelled as he got out of the truck. "Where's Kris?"

"Wes, what the hell is going on tonight?" Brian asked. "Kris showed up at the restaurant as I was leaving in tears and asked me to take her home."

"Did you take her home? To my house?"

"No, Karen was here at my place. She had driven Kris to the game to watch you tonight. Nice game, by the way," Brian added.

"Brian, not now," Wes said in an annoyed tone. "Where is Kristin?"

"I brought her back here," Brian said.

Wes started up the path towards Brian's apartment.

"She's not here, Wes," Brian yelled.

"You just said she was here," Wes said. "Can't anyone just give me a straight answer tonight?"

"She was here to see Karen. She told Karen what happened, puked in my car, and Karen took her back to her house."

"Okay, great," Wes said, moving back towards his truck. Wes peeked his head over the roof of the truck before he got in.

"Kris puked in your car?" Wes asked. "Why?"

"How should I know? All I wanted to do was come home and have sex with my fiancée, and all this happened."

"Too much information, Brian," Wes said. "Thanks for your help. Good luck with the car. Tell me the bill to go have it detailed."

Wes sped off back towards Chandler, not caring about speed limits, red lights, or traffic. His only goal was to find Kristin.

****

Wes arrived outside of Karen's house about forty minutes and one speeding ticket later. His truck came to a stop right behind Karen's car in her driveway. Wes sprinted up the walkway, reached the front porch, and knocked furiously on the front door.

Karen appeared moments later wearing her robe.

"Wes, she doesn't…"

"Karen, I don't care, you have to let me in so I can talk to her."

Wes tried to push his way past Karen to get inside the house, but Karen shoved him back.

"Wes, I love you, I really do, but you try that again, and I'll have to slug you. I have three brothers, and I kicked all their asses regularly, so I can take you. You and I both know it."

Wes looked Karen over and could see her seriousness.

"Come here," Karen said quietly, getting Wes to follow her over to a couple of wicker seats on the porch.

"What happened?" Karen asked.

"I don't know," Wes said, putting his head in his hands. "We had a great night, I went out to get ice cream, and when I got back, Kris was gone, and this crazy woman Sabrina was in my room. She said she convinced Kris that the two of us were fooling around so Kris would leave and she could be with me. The woman is nuts. She works for the team and has been coming onto me since we met. You must believe me, Karen. I would never do anything to hurt Kris, ever."

"I know you wouldn't, Wes," Karen told him.

"How am I going to fix this?" Wes said, getting up from the chair and pacing around, creaking porch boards along the way.

"Well, you aren't going to fix it tonight," Karen answered. "Go back to Washington, and we'll figure something out."

"We'll figure it out?" Wes questioned.

"You clearly can't do this by yourself, my friend." Karen led Wes down the porch. "Give me a day to see how things go. Play your game tomorrow, and I'll let you know what I come up with."

"Okay, thanks Karen," Wes replied and walked back to his truck.

Wes took his time going back to Washington. The entire ride he pondered the day's events, and how they had gone from so good to so awful in a matter of minutes.

20

Kristin awoke in the morning hoping the night before was nothing but a bad dream, but she realized when she saw her yellow dress hanging on the back of the bedroom door that it had all happened. All through her shower and when she dressed, she went over the details as she sought to decipher what went wrong and how Wes betrayed her like that.

Kristin got downstairs and saw Karen in the kitchen, fixing coffee.

"Coffee, Champ?" Karen asked, holding up a mug.

"Thanks," Kristin said. She took the cup and sat down at the kitchen table. Karen looked over at Kristin and saw her fidget in the chair, rolling her head back and forth on her shoulders.

"You okay?" Karen asked.

"I just didn't sleep well, I guess. My neck, back, and shoulders all hurt. I feel miserable."

"Kris, why don't you take today off, call in sick. It was rough yesterday."

"I can't Karen," Kristin said, as she sipped the coffee. "I have a board meeting today at 3. We're finalizing everything about the fundraising dinner, which is tomorrow, then I have Izzy's opening night on Thursday, and your wedding is Friday. There's too much going on."

"That's why you need some me time," Karen advised. "Just take the morning off and come in for the board meeting. I can cover what's going on at the library. Besides, after tomorrow, I am off to get ready for… MY WEDDING!" Karen shouted, making jazz hands.

Karen's actions brought a smile to Kristin's face.

"Okay, you cover the morning, and I'll go to the board meeting," Kristin agreed.

"It will be fine," Karen said. "Besides, we have all the part-timers working for the next few days to cover for us. There's plenty of help. Go take a walk. It's beautiful out. Or go back to bed and take a nap."

"I'll do something, I promise."

Karen walked over and gave Kristin a kiss on the top of her head.

"Okay, see you later," Karen said as she grabbed her bag and walked out of the house.

Kristin sat and sipped her coffee for a while, walking out to the front porch to listen to the birds chirp and feel the warmth of the sun. She looked at her phone a couple of times and saw countless messages from Wes, but she deleted them without listening to them.

When she finished her coffee, Kristin took Karen's advice and went for a walk. She had put on her white and blue floral dress, which seemed ideal for this warm May day. Kristin walked around town, something she did not do very often. She window shopped at some stores and spent some time in the florist smelling the latest flowers and bouquets and talking to the owner about the flowers for Karen's wedding.

Kristin left the flower shop and felt the stiffness in her neck again. It was then she noticed the shingle hanging outside a place up the street that read Dr. Richard Trainor, Chiropractor. Kristin took a few tentative steps down the sidewalk, stopped herself, and then started up again with conviction and walked right into Dr. Trainor's office.

Kristin shut the door quietly since she heard nary a noise in the office. She peeked around the corner and into the waiting room and didn't see anyone. There wasn't even anyone at the receptionist desk.

"Hello?" Kristin said, hearing her voice echo.

"One second," she heard in reply. A moment later, Dr. Trainor popped out from behind the door that led to the exam area.

"Kristin, what a pleasant surprise," Dr. Trainor said with a smile.

"I'm sorry, Dr. Trainor if you're not open..." Kristin said as she started to turn back towards the door.

"No, it's fine," Dr. Trainor remarked. "My office hours are later today. My receptionist Robin doesn't come in for another hour or so. Please, stay, and call me Richard."

"I don't want to bother you if you're not seeing patients," Kristin added. "I just thought, well, I've had some pain and stiffness and..."

"Come on back," Richard said with a smile as he held the door open.

"Are you sure? I don't have an appointment or anything."

"It's fine," Richard offered, picking up a clipboard.

He opened the door to one of the exam rooms, and Kristin saw the padded table in the center of the room. Richard then handed her the clipboard.

"Okay, just fill this out the best you can so I can get an idea of your medical history and what's wrong, and then we'll get started. I'll be back in a moment," Richard left the office, closing the exam room door as he went.

Kristin worked through the forms, answering questions about the pain she felt and what might be causing it. She simply answered "stress" and went on to answer other questions about her activity levels and health.

The door clicked open and startled Kristin as Richard walked through.

"All done?" Richard asked, and Kristin handed over the clipboard.

"Okay, now I'm just going to do a few basic general tests, no big deal."

Richard checked her blood pressure, which he noted was a little high, and then held Kristin's wrist in his hand to check her pulse.

"Your pulse is racing," Richard said quietly.

"I guess I'm a little nervous," she answered.

"Nothing to be nervous about," Richard replied. He picked up his stethoscope off the table and put it in his ears. "I just need to listen to your respiration. Breathe normally," he asked, placing the stethoscope on her back.

Kristin inhaled and exhaled a few times as Richard moved the stethoscope around, but he surprised Kristin when he moved to her front, placing the stethoscope just over her right breast.

"Good," Richard said, putting the scope down. He then wheeled over a stool and sat in front of Kristin.

"I need to check your reflexes," he said and used his small hammer on her hands and arms first.

"Can you lift up your dress a little bit," Richard asked bluntly.

"What? Why?" Kristin asked.

Richard chuckled.

"So I can check the reflexes in your knees, of course."

"Oh, right, sorry," Kristin said, feeling embarrassed.

"It's fine," Richard said as he watched Kristin pull up the hem of her dress slightly so he could check.

"Your reflexes are great," Richard said, standing up.

He picked up Kristin's forms and read them over and then looked at her.

"You say you're having neck, shoulder, and upper back pain? And it's caused by stress?"

"Well, yes, I have a lot going on right now between the library, the fundraising dinner…"

"Oh, right, that's tomorrow. I'm really looking forward to it," Richard commented.

"Right… and then I have Karen's wedding, and Izzy's in the school musical…"

"Who's Izzy?" Richard questioned.

"Oh, Isabelle, that's my boyfriend's daughter… I mean he's kind of my boyfriend… I don't know right now," Kristin said, exasperated.

"Things not going well?" Richard said, as he moved behind Kristin and put his hands on her neck to check it.

"It's… it's a long story with a lot going on," Kristin explained. "No need to bore you with details. Ohhh, that feels good," Kristin said from what Richard did to her neck.

"You certainly have a lot of tension here," Richard said. "Why don't you lie down on the table, face down so I can check your back."

Kristin laid down and felt Richard's hands work down from her neck to her shoulders. He kept massaging her muscles, loosening them and making her feel more relaxed. She could feel the tension melting away and closed her eyes.

"Kristin, I just need to unzip the back of your dress to get to your upper back, okay?"

Kristin just mumbled a "Hmm hmm," without thinking much about it.

She heard the familiar sound of the zipper going down and then felt Richard's hands working on her back, feeling around her spine and then felt him push, and she heard a "pop." Kristin felt instant relief and let out a small groan.

Richard kept up his work, but then suddenly, Kristin felt him unhook the back of her bra. Her eyes flew open, and she asked, "What... what are you doing?"

"I'm sorry, it was in the way," Richard explained. "I needed to get in here," and Richard worked the area with another "pop," that provided more relief.

Kristin was just getting comfortable with the adjustments and feeling great when she felt Richard's left hand slide down from her back to the inside of the front of her bra, cupping her breast. Kristin bolted up on the table and pushed him away.

"What was that?" Kristin yelled.

"Oh, come on, Kristin, you know what that was," Richard laughed.

"It was inappropriate is what it was," she said. She climbed off the exam table and struggled with her bra to hook it up again.

"Really? You've spent weeks flirting with me to get what you want for the library, and then you come in here when you know there's no one here, telling me about the problems you have with your boyfriend, that you feel tense, and then all that moaning on the table. It all seems obvious to me."

"If you misinterpreted all those things, I'm sorry, but I never intended any of that. And if this is how you treat your patients than maybe the police need to hear about this." Kristin zipped up the back of her dress and stormed out of the office.

"Think about what you're doing Kristin," Richard said, following her out. "I can certainly make a case to the board that you are not fit to work at the library anymore."

"What are you talking about?"

"Everything I just said to you – how you flirted and came on to me to get my vote on the board, how you convinced me to get you grants and more funding and you do God knows what with the money, how you came here to seduce me, missing time at work all the time, like right now – there are a lot of coincidences that can be pretty compelling."

"None of that is true," Kristin said. "No one will believe you."

"You think so?" Richard raised an eyebrow. "I was able to convince Marion Harris that I really wanted to be on that boring library board, wasn't I? I just wanted to be on there to get a chance with you."

"You're disgusting," Kristin said.

"Don't do anything rash, Kristin," Richard warned, holding her arm and then caressing her fingers with his. "Everything has consequences."

Kristin yanked her hand away and stormed out of the office, racing down the sidewalk until she stood in front of the police station. She stayed motionless for a minute or two before Officer Nash, one of the females on the force who was just walking in, saw Kristin and stopped.

"Hi Kris," she said but got no reaction. Officer Nash turned back around and looked at Kristin. "Kristin, you okay?"

Kristin blinked a few times and then thought through what she should do.

"Hi Beth, yeah, I'm fine," she said, smiling. "I was just zoning out. I've got a lot on my plate lately. I'll see you later."

"Sure thing," Beth told her. "Say hi to Wes for me. Hell of a game last night."

"Right, I'll let him know," Kristin said as she walked off towards the library.

She felt like she needed Wes now more than ever but didn't know if he was the answer either.

21

Kristin sat through the board meeting, barely uttering a word. The whole time she kept looking over at Richard Trainor, thinking about what he had done, how he had acted and behaved, and what he had said. Kristin couldn't tell the police, Marion, or anyone on the board without him putting up a fuss and lying to get himself out of trouble and to ruin her in the process. Before Kristin knew it, the meeting was over.

"So, I guess we'll see everyone at the dinner tomorrow," Marion said, closing her portfolio. "Kristin, is Wes going to make it?"

"Yes Kristin, will he be there?" Richard said. "I would love to get to meet him."

"I don't think he'll make it," Kristin said solemnly. "He has a game in the afternoon."

"Oh, that's too bad," Marion said, standing up.

Everyone filed out of the room, with Richard walking out behind Kristin.

"If you need an escort to the party, I would be happy to take you," Richard whispered to her.

"Stay away from me," Kristin hissed.

"Temper, temper, Ms. Arthur. You know your mood swings lately are really affecting your job performance. Something else I may need to bring up with Marion."

Kristin marched out of the building and went to the library right away. Karen was there at the counter, but there wasn't another soul in the place.

"Try to work your way through the crowd, Kris," Karen kidded.

"Not now, Karen," Kristin said as she stormed into her office.

"Now what?" Karen said.

Kristin shot Karen a look of disdain.

"I'm sorry that came out the wrong way," Karen said, sitting down. "What's going on?"

"Richard Trainor is what's going on," Kristin spat out. "That lying, backstabbing, blackmailing, groping asshole…"

"Whoa, you never swear," Karen said. "What did he do?"

Kristin explained the predicament with Richard Trainor and how she didn't see any way out of it.

"I knew I didn't like that guy the minute I saw him," Karen snapped. "We need to tell Marion, or the police, or both."

"He'll just deny everything, Karen, and turn it back on me. He already said as much. I don't see any way out of this. Maybe I'm just better off quitting and going back home to Georgia. I've managed to mess everything up here. I might just need a new start somewhere else."

Karen walked over and gave Kristin a hug.

"You're too much of a northerner now to go back to Georgia," a voice said from outside the office door.

Kristin looked up and saw Wyatt Martin standing there in his cowboy hat. He took his hat off when he walked in the office.

"What is all this that is going on around here?" Wyatt asked. "Between you, Wes, Izzy, Jenny, Karen and Brian, it's like a dang soap opera or romance novel around here."

"Did you hear all that?" Kristin asked.

"Enough of it to know that Richard Trainor needs some straightening out," Wyatt offered.

"Wyatt don't do anything crazy," Kristin warned. "He's a big, strong guy and he'll just say he didn't do anything."

"Big strong guys don't scare me much, Kristin. I've been kicked in the chest by horses twice as big and strong as him. Besides, I have back up," Wyatt said with a smile.

"Back up?" Kristin asked.

Wyatt stepped back out into the library and waved his arm, and Wes walked over.

"Wes, what are you… why are you here?" Kristin said, unsure of how to react.

Wes started to say something before Wyatt stepped in.

"Before you say anything son and put your foot in your mouth, let me say my piece, please? Kristin, I may not be the smartest man in town. I never went to college and barely got out of high school. I know farming and horses, and I know something else – that Wes is an honest man who would never do anything to hurt you. I've seen him with his first wife and all he went through, and he loved her despite it all. With you…"

"Dad, please let me finish this," Wes interrupted. He walked in front of Kristin and took her hands. "Kris, with you, it's a thousand times different. You make me a better person in every way. Before you came along, I didn't realize how empty my life was, and I would never do anything to mess that up. Have I made mistakes lately, you bet. I should have been honest with you about wanting to play again. But one mistake I would never make is cheating on you. I had nothing to do with that woman – I never have and never will, and you must believe that. You're the only person for me, and without you, I don't know where I'll be."

Kristin stood silent for a minute, looking into Wes' eyes and seeing the sincerity and love that was there. She broke into a smile and squeezed Wes' hands.

"Don't just stand there, boy, kiss her!" Wyatt told Wes.

Wes took Kristin in his arms, and they kissed passionately while Karen and Wyatt looked on.

"Okay, the show's over now," Wyatt said, clapping his hands. "Wes, let's go show this chiropractor what happens when you mistreat a lady."

"Dad, that's not really the answer, and you know it," Wes said.

"So, what do we do?" Karen asked.

"I have an idea," Wes said, putting his arm around Kristin.

22

Angelo's was jam-packed for the fundraising dinner, with everyone dressed in their most elegant attire. Angelo had arranged quite a spread and pulled out all the stops, with his chefs crafting dinners that looked almost too good to eat. Board members milled about the room, talking to the potential donors in the town. Kristin was a focal point, trying to explain to many people how their donations can help make a significant difference not just to the library, but to the town and its future.

Kristin looked stunning in her dark blue strapless, fitted gown, and she turned many heads, including that of Richard Trainor. Kristin tried to keep her distance from him, spending time talking to other guests or sitting with Karen and Brian, who both were in attendance despite their wedding just two days away.

"I'm going to the bar to get a drink," Brian said. "Do you ladies want anything?"

"A cosmopolitan for me, baby," Karen said with a wink.

"Kris?" Brian asked.

"Oh, just a ginger ale for me, Brian, thanks," she said.

"You got it."

Brian wandered off towards the bar while Kristin looked around nervously.

"What is it with you and the ginger ale?" Karen asked.

"I'm trying to lay off the alcohol, Karen, and I like ginger ale, for your information. Besides, I'm nervous. Maybe it will settle my stomach."

"Don't worry, everything will be fine," Karen replied.

"He keeps staring at me," Kristin told Karen, referring to Richard.

"Well, number one, he's a pervert," Karen said. "Number two, have you seen you in that dress? You look amazing."

"Thanks," Kristin said as she smoothed her hands over her dress. "Wes picked this one out for me."

"Well he has good taste," Karen said. "I should have taken him dress shopping with us for the wedding."

Brian returned with the drinks, and Kristin took a big sip of her ginger ale.

A clinking of glass on glass could be heard towards the center of the room, and there Marion Harris stood, rapping a fork on her champagne glass to get everyone's attention.

"Folks, I just want to thank you all for coming out tonight to support our efforts with the library, and hopefully we can make this year even better than last. I want to say a special thanks to our librarian, Kristin Arthur, without whom none of this would possible. Kristin, your tireless efforts have made our library one of the finest in the county, and we all thank you."

The crowd gave a big round of applause, and Kristin gestured an embarrassed wave as a thank you.

"Now," Marion continued, "Angelo and his staff have put together this amazing feast for us, so please go to your tables and enjoy!"

Guests dispersed to their assigned tables, and Kristin nodded to Karen, indicating she was going to go to the ladies' room before sitting down to eat.

Kristin got to the short hallway where the restrooms were, but before she could go into the ladies' room, Richard took her by the arm.

"Where are you rushing off to?" he asked her.

"The bathroom, if you must know," she said, tugging her arm free.

"You know, this doesn't have to be as difficult as you're making it, Kristin," Richard remarked. "We could have a lot of fun together. I'm a wealthy man, not ballplayer rich like your sports star ex-boyfriend, but I do well. Play ball with me and keep quiet and I think you'll find I could make you happy instead of making your life miserable."

"What do you mean, play ball with you?" Kristin asked, touching Richard's arm.

"I mean, forget about what happened in my office. Stop thinking about it and what I did. I was just trying to help you, you know, relax. We can do some great things in this town. I can make sure you get everything you want for the library and more. Those geezers on the board can be swayed by anything. All it takes is just the right words and touch."

Richard's finger caressed Kristin's bare arm and worked up towards her shoulder until his hand was behind her head. He leaned in to try to kiss her, but Kristin pulled back.

"It's funny that you asked me to play ball, Richard," Kristin whispered, her lips almost touching his.

"Why is that?" he asked, moving towards her again.

"Playing ball is more of my thing," Wes said from behind Richard. Wes was standing in the men's room door, staring down Richard.

"Oh, Richard, you haven't met Wes Martin. Wes, this is Dr. Trainor, the one I told you about," Kristin said with a stern look.

"Right, the chiropractor, I remember you mentioning him," Wes said. Wes moved towards Richard menacingly.

"Hey, I don't know what she told you," Richard said, stepping backward. "But I didn't do anything. I was completely professional."

"It's completely professional to put your hands all over me, grope my breasts, and then blackmail me to get me to have sex with you so I can keep my job?" Kristin yelled, drawing attention from others in the room.

"None of that happened," he shot back. "You can't prove it either."

"Funny, you just confessed to stuff right here in the hallway," Wes said to him.

"I don't remember saying anything like that," Richard said, straightening his bowtie. "Who do you think people are going to believe, a respected doctor, or the librarian with an ax to grind and her washed-up ballplayer boyfriend?"

"You're right, Richard," Kristin said, straightening his bowtie for him and making it tighter.

"Oh, do you like my corsage? White roses, my favorite. Wes got it for me," she said, showing Richard her wrist.

"It's lovely," he guffawed.

"Funny thing about this one," Kristin remarked. "Wes spent a little extra to get one with a microphone in it that transmits to the police car outside."

Kristin peeled back one of the roses to reveal the microphone and smiled.

"You bitch!" Richard screamed, getting everyone's attention as he lunged towards Kristin.

Wes grabbed Richard from behind and pulled him into the men's room. He dragged him over towards the stalls, where Wyatt dutifully held a stall door open. Wes spun Richard around and dunked his head into the toilet, holding him there while Richard thrashed about. Wes pulled Richard's head up, letting him gasp some air, before dunking him down again.

"I think that's enough, son," Wyatt said calmly.

"Are you sure? I think I could do this all night," Wes said, pushing Richard's head further down.

"I can take it from here, Wes," Beth Nash said as she entered the men's room.

Wes released Richard's scalp, and Richard panted for air.

Beth took her handcuffs out and cuffed Richard and began to haul him out of the men's room. When they came out, Kristin was standing there with Karen. Kristin walked right up to Richard and glared at him.

"I would love to take a swing at you right now," Kristin said, "but I'm not going to give you the satisfaction of me putting my hands on you." Kristin walked over and took Wes' hand.

Karen looked at Richard as well.

"I'm not too proud," she said and proceeded to kick Richard Trainor in the groin, causing him to double over. "Have a good night, Dick!" She yelled at him as he crumpled on the floor.

"You really should be more careful, Dr. Trainor," Beth said as she pulled him to his feet. "It's easy to trip and fall in these cuffs."

Kristin turned and gave Wes a big kiss and then led him by the hand out towards the dinner.

"You're amazing," she said to Wes.

"Me? You're the one who got all that out of him," Wes said. "You can be very persuasive when you put your seduction on."

"Oh, you have no idea, Mr. Martin," Kristin said, blowing into Wes' ear. "Maybe you'll find out a little later."

Epilogue

The fundraiser was a huge success, and not because Wes was in attendance. More than one person remarked to Marion Harris how they felt about Kristin and the library and how she was the best thing that ever happened to the library. Tens of thousands of dollars got raised that night, allowing Kristin to move forward with making plans to earmark some of that money for new summer programs, enrichment programs, more activities for seniors, new books, and plenty of other issues.

The next night brought about Izzy's debut as Ariel in the Little Mermaid. Wes managed to convince the Wild Things to give him a few days off so he would be sure to be there for his daughter, and Izzy reserved seats upfront for her father, Kristin, and her grandparents. The high school put on a fantastic show, and the singing, dancing, and costumes were top rate. Izzy got more than one curtain call and a standing ovation when the musical was done. Wes made sure to have a huge bouquet of roses to present to Izzy, and all Izzy could talk about for the rest of the night was how she was looking forward to the shows next year, her senior year in high school.

"Dad," Izzy said over a celebratory pizza party at Wyatt and Jenny's, "this summer there is an acting camp in Pittsburgh. It's six weeks long, and… well, I really want to go."

"I don't know, Izzy," Wes said to her as he picked up a piece of sausage pizza. "Those camps are pretty expensive. I only make $725 a month now. We need to watch what we spend."

Izzy's mouth was wide open as she stared at her father.

"Wesley behave," his mother commented.

"Okay. Let me see the pamphlet, and we'll see what we can work out."

"Thanks, Dad!" Izzy said, kissing him on the cheek before heading off to her room to get the pamphlet.

"You know, if Izzy is away for six weeks, you'll be all alone in that big house while I am playing," Wes said to Kristin. "Maybe you want to come on the road with me for a bit and keep me company. You know, stay in cheap motels, eat fast food, sit on wooden benches in small stadiums. It's pretty swanky. And don't forget Emil will always be around too."

"As tempting as that sounds, I might have to pass," Kristin said, wiping a bit of sauce that sat on Wes' nose with a napkin. "Karen is going to be out for 2 weeks for her honeymoon, and then we have all those new programs starting up. I don't know if I'll have time."

Wes looked disappointed, but Kristin then chimed in.

"I'm sure I can take a week of vacation at some point," she said, elbowing Wes.

****

Friday, May, 22nd was the day of Karen's wedding. Staff, caterers, decorators, and more had spent the hours and days before the wedding prepping the barn and the areas around it to make it all look gorgeous. A large white tent sat outside the barn with the bar and a photo booth for people to pose for pictures. Tables were elegantly decorated throughout the barn, and clear light bulbs had been strung across the entire area. Down by the lake, where the ceremony was, seats had been arranged so that they were facing the archway covered with white flowers that sat in front of the lake. Tiki torches had been placed to light the way as the sun went down, and Brian waited at the archway as Karen rode up in a beautifully arranged carriage that was led by two of Wyatt's most beautiful horses.

Karen and Brian exchanged their vows in front of family and friends, and Kristin smiled proudly as Karen's maid of honor. She gave quick winks to Wes throughout the ceremony as he sat near the front in a debonair black suit. Once the Justice pronounced them man and wife, Karen practically leaped into Brian's arms and kissed him, almost knocking him over into the lake. Kristin went over and gave her best friend the biggest hug possible before the happy couple walked back up the makeshift aisle and into the carriage to head up to the reception.

The crowd steadily thinned out down by the lake as Wes walked over to Kristin, who was watching the carriage disappear up the trail.

"It was a beautiful ceremony," Wes commented, putting his arm around Kristin as they looked out over the lake.

"It sure was," Kristin sighed.

"You did a hell of a job pulling all this together in such a short time. You should be proud of yourself," Wes told her.

"I didn't do that much," Kristin said, playing down her role. "I made some phone calls, set up a few meetings, scheduled decorators, that was about it."

Kristin turned to look out over the lake.

"If I had more time, I think I could have made it even better. This is an ideal spot and has lots of potential. All in all, though, I think it went pretty well."

Kristin watched as some swans swooped down towards the lake and skimmed their way into the water, coming to rest not far from the shore.

"You think you can do better then?" Wes remarked from behind Kristin.

"I'm pretty sure I could," Kristin said. She spun around to look for Wes but didn't see him right away. She glanced downward and saw him down on one knee.

"I know it's not ideal to do this on someone else's wedding day at their wedding, but I couldn't think of a better moment or a more special place for us," Wes said to her. "Kristin, there is no person that I want to spend the rest of my life with, through the good, bad, crazy and everything else, and goodness knows we've had plenty of everything else."

Kristin let out a brief laugh, but tears of anticipation were forming in her eyes.

Wes flipped open the ring box he held in his hand.

"Will you marry me?"

"Yes… yes, I will," Kristin said softly.

Wes stood up so he could place the ring on Kristin's finger, and the two embraced and kissed by the light of the torches and the moon.

"Any thoughts about when you might like to have the wedding?" Wes remarked as the two walked over towards the picnic area that was so special to both of them.

"Hmmm, I'm thinking in the fall, around September," Kristin said as she considered it.

"Really, I would have thought you would want it in the spring or the summer. That's a long time to wait," Wes said.

"Well, the weather will be perfect then, with the leaves changing and all here on the farm. And I want to make sure I can fit into my dress," Kristin said as she walked under the tree nearby.

"What are you talking about?" Wes quizzed. "You can fit into any dress you want, and I don't care about any of that anyway. I'm marrying you, not a dress."

"It's just that if we have the wedding too early in the year, I won't fit into the dress I like, Wes," she emphasized, looking down.

Wes looked down and saw Kristin with her hands rubbing over her stomach, and then looked back up at Kristin.

Kristin smiled and nodded at Wes.

"You're… are you sure? How far along? When did you find out?" Wes rattled off question after question until Kristin put a finger up to his lips.

"I had a pretty good idea when I was getting sick all the time that something was going on, and then when I went to see my doctor, she confirmed it for me. The baby is due in December."

"Kris, that's wonderful!" Wes exclaimed, lifting her off the ground and then putting her back down gingerly. "That's perfect, it will be during the offseason."

Kristin narrowed her eyes.

"Really, that's what you're worried about?"

Wes took Kristin's hand as they started to walk back towards the barn where the reception was.

"Of course not, I was joking," Wes said seriously. "I wouldn't care when the birth is. I'm just glad it's happening."

"So am I," Kristin said. She kissed Wes on the cheek, standing on her tiptoes.

"Sounds like it's going to be a busy year for us," Wes said. "The baby, a wedding, Izzy graduating high school, I hope I can handle all of it."

"We'll manage just fine, Mr. Martin," Kristin added, swinging hers and Wes' hands as they held each other.

"I believe you're right, Ms. Ar… future Mrs. Martin," he corrected.

"Damn right!" Kristin squealed as she ran up the pathway.

Made in the USA
Coppell, TX
11 November 2019